# BROKEN MOON

# BROKEN MOON

JOHN L. LANSDALE

BOOKVOICE PUBLISHING

This book is a work of fiction. All incidents and all characters are fictionalized, with the exception that well-known historical and public figures are products of the author's imagination and are not to be construed as real. Where real-life historical figures appear, the situations and dialogues concerning those persons are fictional and are not intended to depict actual events within the fictional confines of the story. In all other respects, any resemblance to persons living or dead is entirely coincidental.



ISBN
978-1-949381-34-4 Hardcover
978-1-949381-35-1 eBook

BookVoice Publishing
PO Box 1528
Chandler, TX 75758
www.bookvoicepublishing.com

# JOHN L. LANSDALE TITLES

-Broken Moon
-The Last Good Day
-Long Walk Home
-Beyond Imagination
-Kissing the Devil
-Slow Bullet
-The Complete Files of Detective Thomas Mecana
-Horse of a Different Color
-When the Night Bird Sings
-Twisted Justice
-The Box
-Zombie Gold
-Emergency Christmas
-Hell's Bounty [with Joe R. Lansdale]
-Tales from the Crypt (Comic Series)
-That Hellbound Train (Graphic Novel)
-Yours Truly, Jack the Ripper (Graphic Novel)

"Mickey Spillane fans will welcome this page-turner...Lansdale effectively delays revealing the novel's big secret until the end. Those who like their thrillers with a heavy dose of violent action will be satisfied." - **Publishers Weekly review of *Slow Bullet***

"This is an entertaining, science fiction-historical-horror blend with resourceful protagonists and a solid cast of secondary characters."
**- Booklist review of *Zombie Gold***

"*Slow Bullet* is a straight-ahead thriller...it's about action, and there's plenty of that. Check it out." - **Bill Crider's Pop Culture Magazine**

"...the author's innate ability to spin a complex tale painted with vivid characters and intense suspense provides readers with a well-paced book that they may find difficult to set down...a worthwhile suspenseful ride." - **Amazing Stories review of *Horse of a Different Color***

"Has something for everyone... It's exciting, entertaining and educational. A fun ride."
**– TV personality Joan Hallmark, review of *Zombie Gold***

"...something unique and comfortable and difficult to put down. Highly recommended." – **Cemetery Dance review of *Hell's Bounty***

"True to Lansdale tradition, John L. Lansdale has compiled a piece of work that should appeal to a wide range of readers."
**– Amazing Stories review of *Zombie Gold***

"*Long Walk Home* really touched and gripped me. A great bittersweet story of light and shadow about growing up in a time gone by. I loved it." – **author Joe R. Lansdale**

*Always For Mary*

*The logic of a mad man is a sane man's confusion.*
Joe R. Lansdale

# 1

Dust was stirred up so thick you couldn't tell how many horses had chased Marshal Lamont Dobbs into the corral. A bullet dropped the marshal's horse before he reached the barn. He tried to pull his Winchester out of the saddle scabbard but his horse had fallen on it and bullets were getting too close. He drew his six-gun and caught a charging horse with a quick shot. The rider went over the horse's head as it went down and the rider rolled behind a water trough.

The marshal ran into the barn in a cloud of dust, pulling the doors shut.

The rider thrown from the horse yelled out from behind the water trough, "We got you pinned down, Marshal. You and your gal are good as dead."

A shot from the house nearby put a bullet hole in the water trough, water squirting out of the hole

"Hope she got you, Jeb," the marshal yelled.

"I'm fine. It's you that's done for. You hung my pa, Marshal. Ain't no forgivin' that."

"He had it coming. All you Snyders are horse thieves."

"Me and my brothers are going to enjoy killing you and having some fun with your kid 'fore we kill her. Never had a Cheyenne or a half-breed. Wanted you to know before you die."

"Billie Jo's got nothin' to do with this! Leave her alone," the marshal yelled. He checked his .44 and his belt. He had six rounds and no way to get the Winchester.

The barn door flew open and a saddled multi-colored paint mare came running out. The marshal ran behind her and fired a shot at the water trough, pieces of wood peeling off the top. He heard a painful "damn you" from behind the water trough.

Snyder was poking his head out too far from a pine tree when Billie Jo ran from the house and shot him between the eyes with her Winchester. The others hunkered down out of sight. She jumped in the paint's stirrup with her left boot, grabbed the reins and swung her body into the saddle, firing the Winchester in all directions as she whirled the horse around.

"Go to the Judge," the marshal yelled at Billie Jo as he fired his last bullets at the other Snyders. A barrage of bullets from four Snyder guns ripped holes in his shirt. He fell to the ground, dead.

Billie Jo kicked her horse to a full gallop, jumped the corral fence and headed for Rainbow Peak, Kansas, bullets whizzing by her as she rode.

Jeb came out from behind the water trough, pulling splinters out of his face, and walked directly to the marshal. He placed the barrel of his .44 against the marshal's badge and pulled the trigger—blowing a hole in the badge and into the marshal's chest.

He mounted his dead brother's horse. "We'll come back and bury Seth," Jeb said and they all rode after Billie Jo, two headed across Sunset Mountain on a shortcut to Rainbow Peak while the other two continued to ride after her across barren ground into the sun.

Billie Jo rode up on the top of a knoll, watching them riding hell-bent for leather toward her. After dismounting, she plucked a sunflower from the ground and blew the petals, taking note of the wind speed and direction.

The Snyder brothers were making up ground to her fast. She turned the paint sideways, took her Winchester from the saddle scabbard and laid it across the saddle. The sun struck the gun barrel, sending a ray of light down the dell. She pulled her hat down to shade her eyes, aimed and fired. The lead rider fell from his horse almost a hundred yards away. The other one stopped, dismounted and scrambled into a small depression. The two going up Sunset Mountain heard the shot, stopped, held their hats between them and the sun, looking back down the mountain to where their brothers were riding to see if the one she shot would get up. He didn't.

She stuck the rifle back in the scabbard, swung up in the saddle and rode as hard as her mare could go, heading for the Judge at the Gallop Saloon in Rainbow Peak.

The killing of another brother had slowed the Snyders down. They dropped back out of range as she rode on. They picked up their dead brother and laid him across his saddle as she disappeared over the hill.

When Billie Jo rode up to the Gallop Saloon the sun was on the other side of noon above a snow-covered mountaintop on a Thursday in May of 1876. The wind had died down and left the dirt streets like they had been swept with a broom. The Judge's Appaloosa was tied to the hitching post. The town was bustling with people everywhere except the saloon, too early for most. A sign on the wall by the swinging doors of the saloon read CIRCUIT COURT JUDGE FULLER G. NEWTON.

She jumped off the mare, wrapped the reins around the hitching post, pulled the Winchester from the saddle scabbard, stepped up on the boardwalk, pushed the swinging doors open and hurried in. The only people in the saloon were the Judge; his hired hand, Digger; his bartender; a couple men playing cards with the local drunk; and a working girl named Loretta.

Everyone watched as Billie Jo walked across the floor to the table. One of the card players was Steamboat, a big broad-shouldered man with long, bushy black hair and a full beard so thick he looked like a grizzly bear. The one beside him was Eddie, a big muscled-up blacksmith. The Judge had his back to the wall. He could see Billie Jo straight-up and was also staring at her figure in the bar mirror as she walked toward him. Her long black hair and fiery black eyes mirrored the beauty of her Cheyenne mother, while the Colt strapped to her hip was from her marshal father.

"Billie Jo Dobbs, your pa don't allow you in here," the Judge said, twisting in his chair and cutting his deep-blue bloodshot eyes up at her. "Your daddy is going to be pissed at me big time."

"The Snyders ambushed Pa and me on account of you hangin' old man Snyder," Billie Jo said. "Pa's dead. I got two Snyders and slowed 'em down a bit. The other three are comin' after me. I'm goin' to kill ever damn one of 'em."

"Sorry to hear 'bout your pa, girl," the Judge said. "He was a good man."

The two card players nodded in agreement. The Judge and players laid their cards on the table.

"Go ahead and cry if you want to," Eddie the blacksmith said.

"Papa said never cry, said it shows weakness."

The Judge sighed and brushed his hand through his long pepper-gray hair, then put on his black hat and wiped whiskey off his thick mustache with the back of his arm.

"He was a special man," the Judge said, adjusting his red suspenders over his stained white cotton shirt on his lean, tall body and pushed his Colt down on his hip.

Billie Jo dropped her head to hide a tear.

"Won't be long 'til we'll have to kill 'em," the Judge said. He picked up the eight-gauge shotgun off the table, checking the loaded breech, walked over behind the bar and picked up eight more shells he stuck in his pockets. Cradling the shotgun, he walked over to his hired hand, Digger, sitting at a table by himself, his long legs stretched out with his feet in a chair, snoring, his hat pulled down over his eyes with shaggy blonde hair poking out the sides.

The Judge kicked his feet off the chair. "Wake up, boy."

Digger fell out of the chair onto the floor. "What the hell," he said.

"Billie Jo's pa has been killed by the Snyders, now they comin' after Billie Jo. That means us too, get your rifle."

Digger looked up and saw Billie Jo. "Sorry," he said. "Really sorry to hear that."

Billie Jo was holding back tears, too choked up to speak, but nodded a thank you.

Ernest, the old bartender with a thin wrinkled face and white hair, stopped wiping a glass to stare at Billie Jo. He picked up a twelve-gauge from under the bar, loaded it and laid it on the bar.

"I'm ready, Judge," Ernest said.

"Good. Carl Snyder had it comin'," Judge Fuller said. "Him and his five boys was stealing horses from the Indians and selling them to the Army. Nobody cares about the Indians' ponies, but they stole two of Buck Claremore's branded horses a couple weeks ago and sold them to the Army. The Army insisted I hang the stupid sonsabitches."

"You don't care about the Indians, Judge?" Billie Jo asked.

"I can't do nothing for them. The Army don't want the horses as much as they do getting them from the Indians. Eddie, you and Steamboat hold your right hand up."

"What for?" Steamboat said.

"I'm going to make you deputies," the Judge said. "There's rifles behind the bar."

"I ain't got nothin' against the Snyders," Eddie said.

"Me neither," Steamboat said. "Plus, I had a full house."

"I don't give a shit, raise your hand."

Eddie and Steamboat looked at each other, shaking their heads no.

"Do it," the Judge said in a stern voice, "or I'll arrest you for contempt of court."

They each raised their hands.

"I, Judge Fuller G. Newton, do hereby appoint you deputy marshals for as long as needed. I'll give you ten dollars and a free visit with Loretta for your help."

"That's better," the blacksmith said. "We get a badge?"

"No, you don't need one."

"I didn't say they could have a free one," Loretta said.

"What? You do what I tell you. I own the damn place," Fuller said.

"Let them do her," Loretta said, pointing at Billie Jo. "Her problem."

"No. You'll get two dollars apiece, like you always do."

"You get half back?" Loretta said.

"Not this time. Digger, go take the horses down to Eddie's shop 'fore the Snyders get here and pass the word around town what's going on. It's between the Snyders and the law."

"I don't want to be out there with the Snyders coming," Digger said. "They're meaner than a rattlesnake."

"It'll cost you for the feed," Eddie said.

"Then I'll keep the money from their horses after we kill 'em," Judge Fuller said. "Digger, get your ass out there and do what I told you." He cradled the shotgun in his arms. Steamboat looked at the double-barrel.

"That an eight-gauge?" he asked.

"Yeah, it can blow out a wall," Fuller said.

"Don't doubt that, I only seen two in my life."

"Last owner of this one 'fore me was Jack Morgan. I snuck up on him and put a .45 Remington shot in the back of his head. He never knew what hit him."

"Terrible, to do something like that," Steamboat said.

"He was an outlaw. I'm more befitting to own it than he was. Even gave it a name: Big Boy, in remembrance of ol' Jack."

Digger walked to the swinging doors, looked out and hurried to the horses.

Billie Jo rolled the cylinder of her six-shooter across her arm to see if it was fully loaded, spun it around on her fingers a couple of times and dropped it back in the holster with a smooth motion.

Steamboat was watching Billie Jo. "You see that? Never seen a female that familiar with a six-gun, especially one that young."

"Don't piss her off, she might use it on you," Fuller said and grinned. "The marshal taught her what she knows about guns. Army murdered her Cheyenne mama when she was eight, lost her brother to the Indians and growed up here. Now get a rifle and cover a window. And Ernest, get Willie out of here."

"Okay, I'll have to coax him a little," Ernest said.

"Whatever, just get him out of here, he'll be in the way."

Ernest walked over to the table where Willie, the local drunk, was sitting with his head on the table, asleep. Ernest shook him vigorously.

"Wake up, Willie, and get out of here. I'll give you this." Ernest held out a bottle of whiskey. Willie grunted, turned his head toward Ernest and saw the whiskey bottle through his sleepy eyes, licked his lips, sat up and reached for the bottle.

"Get out now and you can have it," Ernest said, pulling it away. Willie pushed his skinny body up from the table, grabbed the whiskey bottle with one hand and held his ragged pants up with the other, and staggered out the doors, holding the bottle like it was a baby.

"Loretta, you and Ernest get upstairs and stay 'til this is over," Judge Fuller said.

"I'm ready to fight, got my shotgun loaded," Ernest said.

"Go on up the stairs, in case they try to get through the bedroom windows," Fuller said.

"Okay. Come on Loretta." Ernest picked up the shotgun and they both started up the stairs.

A rugged-looking old cowboy came running down the stairs carrying his boots, his shirt tail hanging out of his pants.

"I just heard about the Snyders," the man said. "I ain't gettin' killed by them." He ran through the swinging doors out into the street.

"Where did that crazy bastard come from?" Fuller said.

Loretta stopped at the top of the stairs. "He was with me last night. I left him in bed this morning."

"Get your ass out of sight," Fuller said. He then turned to the men in the saloon. "Everybody ready?"

Everyone looked at him but didn't say a word.

"You better be. We got to fight. Don't have a choice."

"You mean you don't," Steamboat said.

"Shut up or I'll shoot you myself," the Judge said.

# 2

Digger came running through the swinging doors. "I see them coming on a ridge 'bout a half-mile out of town."

"Gonna blow anyone that comes through them doors in half with Big Boy here," Judge Fuller said, holding out the shotgun.

Steamboat threw his rifle down and ran by Digger, headed for the back door. "I ain't getting killed over something that don't concern me. I'm getting back to the river."

"You coward!" Fuller turned toward the back door and pulled the triggers on the eight-gauge, blowing a chunk out of the wall and just missing Steamboat as he ran out the door.

"Damn, Judge," Eddie said. "You don't have to kill 'em."

"I didn't." Fuller dumped the spent shells and reloaded, then went to the swinging doors to look out.

The Snyders were charging into town, bullets hitting the walls. He waited for a rider coming toward him to get in range then turned both barrels loose, cutting down the horse and the rider in the street, both dead. Several people on the street ran for cover.

Steamboat came riding out of the blacksmith shop at a hard gallop. Jeb Snyder swung down from his horse against the saloon wall and knocked Steamboat out of the saddle with his first shot, then made his way on foot down the side of the building toward the saloon doors. All the stores in town had locked up. It was a Snyder Saloon War.

Jeb's brother rode straight through the saloon doors, knocking them off their hinges and Fuller down to the ground, his shotgun flying out of his hands and sliding across the floor. Billie Jo drew her Colt and shot the rider twice before he could pull the trigger once. Jeb ran through the busted window, his face still full of bloody streaks from the splinters in the water trough, and aimed at Fuller. Digger shot him in the chest twice with his Winchester. Jeb dropped his Spenser and on the way down it went off when it hit the floor. A bullet grazed Fuller's left upper arm. Jeb was on the floor gasping for breath when Billie Jo ran over to him with the hammer back on her Colt and aimed it at his heart.

"Your time to die," Billie Jo said.

"Shoot him, Billie Jo! The sonofabitch hit me," Fuller said, holding his bleeding arm.

Billie Jo tightened her finger on the trigger. Eddie pushed the barrel of Billie Jo's Colt away and looked at Jeb. "He's dead," Eddie said. "It's over." He dropped the rifle on the floor and walked out of the saloon.

Billie Jo eased the hammer down and dropped the Colt in her holster. "I got to go get my pa."

"I'll go with you," Digger said. "I owe him. He supplied most of the hombres I dug graves for to make a livin'."

"Billie Jo could use some help," Fuller said, wiping blood off his arm with a bar towel.

"We'll get a wagon from Eddie," Digger said.

Ernest and Loretta came down the stairs. "I'll get something to fix your arm, Judge," Loretta said.

"That would help, before I bleed to death." Loretta got a bottle of whiskey and poured it on his arm. "Shit, that burns. Thought you was going to help. Gimme that damn bottle." He turned the whiskey bottle up and downed what was left, then threw it against the wall, smashing it.

"You got to sterilize it first," Loretta said, staring at him. She tore off a piece of her petticoat, wiped his arm dry and bandaged it.

"Digger, come here," Fuller said.

Digger walked up to him. "What you need, Judge?"

"Real close," Fuller said, motioning with his finger for him to come closer.

Digger put his ear up close to Fuller's mouth and heard him whisper: "You try to get in her pants, I'll cut your dick off."

"For god's sake, I'm trying to help," Digger said.

"You better be."

"Billie Jo, bring Lamont in. We'll bury him in Boot Hill," Fuller said. "Something will chew him up if we don't get him now."

"You goin' to pay for the box, Judge?" Digger said.

"Yeah."

"No," Billie Jo said. "I'll pay for it. He showed me where he hid his grave money."

"He's owed almost a month's pay, you want it now or later?" Fuller said.

"Now."

Fuller sat his shotgun across his lap, gathered the money off the card table and handed it to Billie Jo.

"More there than he was owed," he said.

"Will this cover the cost of that shotgun?" She pointed to the gun in Fuller's lap.

"I suppose so, but I don't really want to sell it."

"I heard you talkin' about it."

"Would knock you down to fire it," he said.

"I don't want to shoot it. Me and Pa was goin' to Cheyenne county. He wanted me to meet my people, see how they lived. Said we should have a special gift for the chief."

"You mean your uncle, Wooden Leg?"

"Yeah, Pa told me all bout him, a brave Cheyenne."

"He won't know you now, can't just walk in, they would burn you alive. Indian or not."

"That's why I wanted it. He would know it was special."

"We can talk about it again later."

"Let's go, Billie Jo," Digger said.

"If they left their brothers there, Digger, you leave them there," Fuller said.

"I can't do that. I got to bury 'em if the buzzards ain't already got 'em."

"You're the one doing the digging, but I ain't goin' to pay you for it."

"Didn't ask you to. We'll be back today."

# 3

Digger and Billie Jo's wagon rolled up to the Gallop Saloon late that afternoon with the late Marshal Lamont Dobbs stretched out in the back with a blanket over his body.

The early morning sun was hanging on the horizon as they stopped at the hitching post. Digger got off the wagon and tied the horses.

Billie Jo was wearing a black dress and no gun belt. She was holding her father's badge, now with a bullet hole in it, in her hand. Digger helped her down from the wagon. They went in the saloon through damaged doors—one hanging sideways by a single nail, the other one on the floor.

People from the saloon and surrounding stores came up to the wagon and pulled back the blanket to take a look at Lamont.

"Glad you're back," Judge Fuller said as they walked up to the bar. "I'm amazed at what you're wearing, Billie Jo, didn't know you had any female things."

"Only this. We put his good boots on him," she said and dropped the badge in her lace-trimmed pocket. "We're going to stop by Eddie's, get a box and take him on up to Boot Hill. Anyone wants to come can."

"One of the Snyders was still out there," Digger said. "I buried him. The place stinks to high heaven."

"They killed Pa's horse and he killed one of theirs," she said. "Buzzards were already on the horses. Don't know what happened to the Snyder I shot on the trail. After the buzzards clean the place up I'm gonna sell it, go to Montana."

"Montana's a long way from Kansas," Fuller said.

"Won't be coming back," she said.

"Why not?"

"Gonna stay with my people."

"They're not your people anymore. You was raised white."

"Then I'll get reacquainted," Billie Jo said.

"Won't work," Fuller said.

"Goin' anyway."

"You would never get there by yourself," Fuller said, "and I don't want to go."

"I didn't ask you to go," Billie Jo said.

"You two are getting on my nerves," Digger said. "Gimme a shot of whiskey, Ernest."

Ernest poured half a glass full of whiskey and Digger downed it with one gulp.

"What'd you do with the dead Snyders in the saloon?" Digger said.

"We put them in the wood shed," Ernest said.

"I'll bury them tomorrow, won't make any difference now."

"An undertaker could get rich here embalming dead folk if we had one," Ernest said. "You and Eddie oughta team up with the boxes and bury people. Goin' to be a lot more in Boot Hill with all the prospectors coming through."

"Nah, tired of burying people. Gonna find me something else to do," Digger said.

"We'll talk bout the Cheyenne later," Fuller said, looking at Billie Jo. He poured himself a shot of whiskey then banged the butt of the shotgun on the bar to get everyone's attention and drank the whiskey.

"We'll have the marshal's funeral 'fore it gets dark," he said. "Lamont was rather fond of whiskey. You can bring it with you if it's alright with Billie Jo."

"Okay with me." She stuck her hand in her dress pocket and squeezed the badge.

"We'll have a toast to him," Fuller said and everyone started grabbing whiskey bottles, heading for the wounded doors.

"Don't have a preacher, Billie Jo," Fuller said. "I got some good things to say about him and some things I better not. After the services you can go down to Mrs. Plat's boarding house for the night. Men might take you for the wrong kind of woman at my place in a dress and you'd kill one or two of 'em."

"Just might," Billie Jo said.

Digger and Billie Jo walked out of the saloon with Fuller and a group of other folks who got on the wagon. They stopped off at the blacksmith and put Lamont in his casket then proceeded on to Boot Hill. The population of Boot Hill was growing faster than the town. Billie Jo held back her tears.

Judge Fuller said his piece, and by the time Digger covered him Boot Hill was full of drunks stopping at Lamont's grave, giving toasts.

"Thank everybody for me, Judge," Billie Jo said. "Pa would have liked the funeral. Gonna go on to the boarding house."

"He would have. I'll tell them and get a cross for the marker."

Digger and Billie Jo rolled on in the wagon and pulled up in front of a two-story well taken care of whitewashed building. A sign over the front porch read:

LADIES OF THE NIGHT - PROFANITY OR SPIRITS NOT WELCOME - WE BELIEVE IN THE LORD

"Forgot how religious they are," Billie Jo said, looking at the sign.

Digger didn't say anything, just wrapped the reins around the brake handle. He knew Homer Plat visited the saloon on a regular basis to be with Loretta. Eda Plat was the only one in town who didn't know. Digger decided he better change the subject.

"Eddie bedded down your horse and fed her. Boy, she sure has beautiful markings and a name I never heard before."

"Yeah, I saw her at a sale in Rainbow Peak when she was about a year old. The black and white colors looked like they were put on with a paintbrush. And my pa gave her the name Bittersweet. She took to me right away, but not to him. According to him, she was bitter to him and sweet to me. That's how she got her name."

"Yeah that's the way females are," Digger said.

"That's just the way men think," Billie Jo said. "Seen you around for several years but don't know much about you."

"Not much to know. Been working for the Judge for about four years. Came in when I ran away from the orphanage up north. Mooched my way here and had to find something to keep from starving to death. The Judge said he could use me for whatever and I've been working for him ever since."

"You know what happened to your family?"

"They was killed by Indians somewhere in Sioux territory on a wagon train when I was a baby. Ran away from the orphanage when I turned sixteen, 'fore they could send me to the army, and eventually I wound up here."

"We're about the same age then," Billie Jo said.

"Yep," Digger said. "I'm twenty, I think."

"You ever go to school?"

"No, but I can read and write. Guess you better get going. I'll get your horse and the rest of your stuff to you in the morning."

"Thanks," she said and stepped down from the wagon. "Hand me the carpet bag."

He picked up the bag and leaned over to her and she took the bag.

"See you in the morning," she said and walked in the boarding house.

Digger wheeled the wagon around and drove on by Boot Hill. He could see drunks passed out all over the place. Eddie was nowhere around at his blacksmith shop.

He unhitched the horses and stood there in amazement, rubbing them down, looking at Bittersweet, thinking it was a miracle Billie Jo and the horse had even survived.

# 4

The next morning, Digger led Bittersweet to the boarding house with the few of Billie Jo's things strapped to the saddle. When he passed Boot Hill, Digger noticed two men were passed out on top of graves. They looked close enough to death to go inside one, he thought.

At the boarding house he saw Homer Plat carrying firewood from outside into the kitchen. Homer was one of those men who looked like he was born for chopping wood—with his bowed legs, barrel chest and big hands.

His wife ran things at the boarding house, including him. She kind of waddled when she walked, with a butt the size of a plow mule. She was the closest thing to a preacher in town but didn't preach anywhere except at the boarding house on Sunday.

Digger tied Bittersweet to the hitching post and went inside.

Billie Jo and some other guest were having breakfast in the dining room. The windows had red checkered curtains and matching tablecloths draped across wooden tables. The swinging kitchen doors were just like the saloon doors, except smaller.

Digger walked up to her table took off his hat. "Good morning, Billie Jo. See you bought some new duds."

"Had to get out of that dress. Used some of the money the Judge gave me. Want some breakfast?"

"Already ate. Your other things and your horse are outside."

"Thanks. I was talking to Mrs. Plat. She said I could get a train ride out of here all the way to Yellowstone with my horse, then go on to Cheyenne on Bittersweet."

"I know you promised your pa, but that train will be taking cowboys and their horses to Yellowstone to round up stray cattle in the area to ship for slaughter as soon as the weather breaks. Not a good place for a woman."

"I can take care of myself."

"Not that good. Marshal Dobbs wanted you to go but he would want you to stay alive more."

"It's my choice, not yours."

"You apparently haven't had much experience with men," Digger said.

"That's none of your business."

A man at a nearby table picked up his beaver hat, pushed his holster back on his hip and turned to Billie Jo.

"Excuse me, ma'am, I couldn't help but overhear. I knew your pa. Name's Slate McGregor."

McGregor was shorter and probably twice the age of Digger, with red hair and beard. He had an ammunition belt across his chest, a double-action Colt on his right hip and a Bowie knife strapped to his left rawhide boot.

"Seen you around before," Digger said. "What're you doing in Rainbow Peak this time?"

"Brought several families in from Billings through Cheyenne country. My pa was a soldier, took a Cheyenne wife, they came up with me."

"What my pa did," Billie Jo said. "When I was eight everything turned sour on my pa, we had to leave the tribe."

"I know. Thought you might need my help if you're going back," Slate said. "Can speak Cheyenne, too."

"I remember a little but not enough. Have a seat, Mr. McGregor."

"Thank you," he said and sat down.

"My pa was killed by some horse thieves."

"I heard when I came in," Slate said. "The young man's right about the train. Some men are always looking for a woman on that train, and they don't care what they have to do to get one. You get on alone, good chance you'll never get off alive."

"That's what I was trying to tell her," Digger said.

"I make my own decisions," Billie Jo said.

"You get on that train, might well be your last decision," Slate said.

"Sounds like you're trying to scare me into hiring you," she said.

"No, ma'am, just telling you the truth," Slate said. "But I am available for a fee if you need help."

"How come you came to the boarding house? Only place I ever seen you before was in the saloon," Digger said.

"I wanted a good meal. The boarding house has the best. My two riders are at the saloon looking for something else. It's a long, lonely ride from Billings, Montana."

"She don't have the money for three gunslingers all the way to Montana," Digger said.

"You don't know what I got, Digger," Billie Jo said.

Slate picked up his hat, stood up, and adjusted his pistol again. "I'll be at the Gallop Saloon if you want to talk some more," he said and walked away.

A round-faced blonde waitress with red ribbons in her pigtails stopped at the table. "Miss Dobbs," she said, "my name's

Bee. Haven't met you but I've seen you around and watched you win the shooting contest last year. I'm very sorry about the marshal. He used to walk me home when I had to work late. I always appreciated it."

"Thank you," Billie Jo said. The waitress smiled and walked away.

Digger didn't want to ask questions about Bee and the marshal so he changed the subject again. "They do have good food here," he said.

"Think I'll stay here for a few days while I figure out what to do," Billie Jo said.

"Don't go," Digger said.

"Don't know yet."

Digger stood up. "Think I'll check in with the Judge. He's expecting a shipment of whiskey coming in on a train today and I still got to fix them swinging doors."

# 5

When Digger walked in the saloon, Slate and his two men were standing at the bar drinking. Digger didn't see the Judge so he walked over to the bar and said hello to Slate and his men. They were all about the same age, maybe Civil War vets ten years ago.

One of the men was Glover, the biggest of the three, with long black hair tied back, almost as long as Billie Jo's, and a scar that looked like a saber mark running down his right cheek to his chin, barely missing his eye. He was carrying two Colts and a Bowie knife.

The other man was known as Hatchet. He was thin with a beard, wearing a hat showing long hair from the left side but none from the other side. A long-handled tomahawk was in his belt with notches on the handle and a Remington Colt on the other side of the belt. A Winchester 73 was leaning against the bar next to his leg.

The three men looked like they were ready for battle. Men in the saloon would glance at them every now and then, sizing them up, but didn't say anything about or to them.

When the cook brought two steaks to a table, Glover and Hatchet carried whiskey to the table to compliment the food.

The thin one was the most resourceful, carrying two full bottles of whiskey, his Winchester 73 and a limp.

Just looking at them, Slate could tell they knew the perils of war. He sat down with them with a whiskey bottle of his own.

"Now this is real food. Not that fancy plate stuff at the boarding house," Glover said, looking at Slate.

"Depends." Slate took a swig of whiskey from the bottle. "There's cowboy style and gentlemen style. I'm the only gentleman," he said and grinned.

"You're the only one that thinks that," Glover said, and he and Hatchet laughed.

Judge Fuller walked in through the repaired swinging doors a few minutes later carrying Big Boy in his right hand, his left hand sticking out of a bandaged left arm. He walked up to Slate.

"I see you're back in town with your partners. Wondered what happen to you."

"Come in from Montana," Slate said. "Gonna leave as soon as we can find a meal ticket."

"How you two doing," Fuller said, looking at Hatchet and Glover.

"Staying alive," Glover said. "Where's Loretta?"

"Probably busy," Fuller said. "Haven't been around this morning. Had to attend to some court business over at Winston. A man shot another man in the back, going to have to hang him."

Just then a train whistle rang out.

"There's our whiskey train, Judge," Digger said. "I'll go unload it." Digger walked out to the train depot across the street.

"That the one that goes to Yellowstone?" Slate said.

"No, that one will be in next week, doesn't always run on schedule," Fuller said. "Hope you're not thinking 'bout riding it."

"Nah, got a trail prospect thinking about it. I'm warning her not to ride it and hire us instead," Slate said.

Fuller glanced over at Glover and Hatchet.

"I'll see if Ernest can locate Loretta."

"You don't get more help, she's gonna wear that thing out," Glover said.

Hatchet didn't say anything, just smiled and kept drinking. Two young farmer-looking men, a big one and a little one, both wearing overalls and clodhoppers, got up from a nearby table and staggered over to Fuller.

"We were listening, Judge," the big one said as he took a drink out of the bottle he was holding.

"You not going to get that nigger a white women, are you Judge?" the little one said then drew a pistol out of his overalls pocket and raised it toward Glover.

Glover stood up, his hand on the butt of his Colt.

Fuller turned to the little one and smashed the shotgun stock across the side of his head. Blood ran down the man's overalls and he fell to the floor, dropping his pistol. Fuller stepped over him and kicked the pistol under a table and stared at the big one.

"You're next if you don't get out of here and take him with you. If you come back I'll kill both of you. You wouldn't make a pimple on that man's ass."

"He was just funning, Judge. He really wasn't going to do anything," the big drunk said.

"Get out," Fuller said. "Take him with you."

Glover stayed in place with his hand still on the Colt.

The big drunk grabbed the little one by the collar and dragged him out the door, blood running down the side of his head.

"That was something to see, Judge," Hatchet said, holding up a bottle of whiskey. "I'll drink to it."

Glover grinned at Hatchet and sat down. "Me too," he said and turned up a glass of whiskey to his lips and drank it.

Fuller looked around the saloon. When he didn't see any more trouble he laid the shotgun on the bar and turned back to Slate.

"Who's your prospect?" Fuller said.

"The marshal's daughter," Slate said. "Talked to her and Digger at the boarding house this morning 'bout the train going to Montana."

"She wouldn't last ten miles on that train," Fuller said. "And she can't pay three hired guns."

"What about you footing the bill, Judge?" Slate said.

"I promised Lamont I would take care of her if something happened to him. It did, so I am. But not to Montana."

"She's goin' to go, I can tell," Slate said. "It's the Cheyenne blood in us. I can see it in her eyes, she's made her choice. We are her best chance at getting there alive."

"You are. If I can't change her mind, we'll talk. But you keep your mouth shut until I have my chat with her."

"Fine with me, Judge," Slate said.

Glover looked at Hatchet, asleep on the table. "Looks like Hatchet's done for the day."

With his head down and hat propped up against the table, Judge Fuller could see the reason Hatchet only had hair showing from under one side of his hat—he had been scalped.

"Got any rooms?" Glover asked.

"Yeah. Enough beds in one room for all of ya'll tonight," Fuller said.

"What about a private one for Loretta if she shows up," Glover said.

Fuller turned to Ernest and told him, "Go check the rooms, all of them. Loretta may be in one."

Ernest sat the whiskey bottles under the bar.

"Follow me, Glover," Ernest said.

Glover corrected Hatchet's hat and picked him up and tossed him on his shoulder with one hand. He picked up Hatchet's rifle with the other hand and headed up the stairs.

"I'll see if I can talk Billie Jo out of this, Slate," Fuller said. "You and the boys can have a free room for a couple days."

# 6

Billie Jo was sitting on her bed, counting the money her father had left her, when a knock on the door surprised her. She flipped the bedspread over the money and opened the door. It was the Bee, waitress.

"Miss Dobbs, Loretta is at the back door to see you," she said. "They won't let her in since she's a lady of the night."

Billie Jo went to the back door and opened it for Loretta, standing on the porch, a scarlet shawl draped around her shoulders. She always thought Loretta was a very pretty woman, just used too much makeup.

"If you come to talk about Pa, I know about you and him," Billie Jo said.

"We were good friends," Loretta said.

"I know what kind of friends you were," Billie Jo said. "Come on in."

Loretta went inside and Billie Jo closed the door. They hurried into Billie Jo's room.

"What do you want with me?" Billie Jo said once they were inside the room.

"I need some help," Loretta said. "My ex-husband Bumper is in town. He showed up at the saloon, told the bartender he was going to kill me. That's not the first time."

"Well ain't nothing right about being a whore but ain't nothing right about someone wantin' to kill you, either. What you want me to do?"

"Wanted to see if I could stay in your room with you until he leaves. I don't have any place to go."

"Why did you leave him?" Billie said.

"I couldn't take the beatings any more. The Judge granted me a separation but Bumper say's he ain't a real judge and that I'm still his wife and he can do whatever he wants to with me, and right now, he wants to kill me. Before your pa was killed, Bumper kept away. He knew the marshal would blow his brains out. Whoring is the only way I know to make a living. You could get rich doing it, the way you look."

"Not for me," Billie Jo said.

"What're you going to do with your pa gone?"

"Goin' to the Cheyenne in Montana."

"Lamont told me bout your mama, he loved her very much. Said she was killed by an army raid when you were eight. That the Cheyenne stole your brother, so he high-tailed it out of there and sent you to Mrs. Goodrich's school to be a teacher. But it looks like you became more of a gunslinger."

"Toting a gun don't have nothin' to do with being a gunslinger," Billie Jo said. "Something I'm good at and it's saved my life."

"What about being a teacher," Loretta said.

"Not my thing. Too confining."

"I would have liked being a teacher. Never had the chance, though."

"Bumper?" Billie Jo said.

"Yeah. I was barely thirteen when my pa sold me to Bumper after meeting him in a saloon down in Dodge, oh, twenty or so years ago. Bumper was twenty. He never let me come to town, just worked me, screwed my ass off and beat me when he felt like it. Even brought over some of his friends once in a while to go to bed with me. Three years ago I ran away, couldn't take it anymore."

"You have any kids?" Billie Jo asked.

"He didn't want any, spaded me like a horse."

"Pa never said anything about him," Billie Jo said. "Tell me more."

"He's a big man—mean—with a quick temper. Big strong hands with arms the size of tree trunks. Always wears overalls and a straw hat. Pretty good with a gun from what I've seen. I think beating me is what he misses the most. His real name is Ben Albright. He's a hard worker, has bumper crops all the time. Maybe that's why they call him Bumper."

"I see why you're hiding out," Billie Jo said.

"Yeah, the whole town knows the boarding house don't allow whores here," Loretta said. "Figured I could be safe here until Bumper went home. His farm is thirty miles from town. That's the only reason I've been able to make it this long, he don't show up too often."

A knock on the door startled them and Billie Jo motioned for Loretta to stand behind the door. She pulled the Colt from its holster hanging on the bedpost. She opened the door and there was Homer.

"Sorry, Miss Dobbs, just lookin' for Loretta," he said. "Don't want no trouble. Bee said she was lookin' for you."

"See what I mean," Loretta said, stepping out from behind the door. "Hello Homer."

"I'm going to have to ask you and Loretta to leave, Miss Dobbs," Homer said.

"You coming over for your visit tonight, Homer?" Loretta said.

Homer stepped inside the room and quickly closed the door. "May the Lord have mercy on your soul, woman."

"He means that, Billie Jo. Every time after we're through he asks Jesus to save me. Nothing 'bout himself, just me."

"Loretta, you're disgusting," Homer said. "Why are you doing this? You want money?"

"She doesn't want money, Mr. Plat. She needs protection."

"You don't let me stay here, Homer, I'm going to pay your wife a visit with details," Loretta said.

"Lordy, Lordy, Lordy," he said. "Keep the door locked and, Loretta, you keep your mouth shut and get out of here as soon as you can. I don't want anyone else to know you're here."

"We don't either," Billie Jo said.

Homer opened the door and hurried out, mumbling to himself.

"I'm going to find the Judge," Billie Jo said. "Stay here, lock the door and don't answer it for anyone but me. You hear?"

"Don't go to the Judge," Loretta said. "If I get you involved, Bumper won't have to kill me because the Judge will. You're his pet."

"Just stay here 'til I get back."

Billie Jo picked up her gun belt hanging on a bedpost, strapped it on and put the Colt in the holster. Then she took her black Stetson off a hook on the door and placed it on her head.

"There's money under the bed spread," Billie Jo said. "Don't be tempted, I know how much is there."

# 7

When Billie Jo walked in the saloon the piano player was playing Garryowen. She saw a man fitting the description of Bumper standing at the end of the bar, guzzling whiskey from a bottle, his sweat-stained old straw hat beside him on the bar.

Digger and Ernest were standing behind the bar at the other end, counting whiskey bottles out of cases with Judge Fuller on a stool writing in a ledger book, his shotgun Big Boy on the bar nearby.

She walked over to the bar and Digger and Ernest nodded and kept counting. She parked on a stool beside Fuller. Several men were following her until they saw where she was going and retreated back to their tables.

"Hi Billie Jo," Fuller said with a smile. "Normally I would ask you to leave the saloon but I'm glad you came by, want to talk to you after I finish this up. Have to count my whiskey, can't trust any of the drummers."

"You know who that big guy is at the end of the bar?" Billie Jo asked.

"Bumper Albright," Fuller said. "That's why I can't find Loretta, she's afraid of him."

"You know that and you let him stay in here?"

"He'll move on soon and Loretta will come back. If I throw him out he gets mad and don't go home and I have to consider killing him. One of these days he's gonna get drunk enough and mad enough I'll have to. For now he's just drinking."

"That's not what she thinks. She's scared to death of him."

"You know where she is?"

"At the boarding house."

"You sneak her in?"

"She came on her own. She told me about the terrible things he did to her."

"Probably no more than most other husbands do to their wives around here," Fuller said.

"Then all of them should be shot. Either you make him leave or I will."

"Now wait a minute, little lady, this is my place and he's not causing any trouble. Only bad thing is Loretta's not working. I'm going to have to hire some more whores somehow."

"Men. None of you have any respect for a woman."

Bumper sat his whiskey bottle on the bar and headed toward Fuller and Billie Jo.

"Oh no," Fuller said to himself. "Hey guys, knock off the counting for a bit. I got something else to handle."

Bumper stopped in front of Fuller and Billie Jo and looked her up and down.

"This some new talent you hired, Judge?"

"You're drunk. Go home," Fuller said.

"I'd be willing to pay top dollar for that."

"Don't get near me, pig," Billie Jo said.

"What's that, you little bitch?" Bumper said.

"Apologize to Miss Dobbs and get out, Bumper," Fuller said, standing up.

"I ain't apologizing. She's the one should be apologizing. Where's that slut Loretta?"

"Get out, Bumper, or they're going to carry you out with a big ol' hole in you," Fuller said and picked up Big Boy off the bar.

Digger walked over beside them. "Why don't you come back another time, Bumper?" he said and smiled.

"Ain't any of your business, boy," Bumper said.

Digger and Ernest sat down the bottles they were holding and backed down the bar. The Piano player quit playing, got off his stool and headed for the back door. It was dead quiet in the saloon. Card players picked up their hands and emptied out into the street with their whiskey.

"You goin' to let that bitch call me a pig, Judge?" He tugged up on his gun belt and stared at Billie Jo.

"You goin' to apologize and leave?" Judge Fuller said, still holding the shotgun. "Last chance."

The three were staring at each other in silence when the swinging saloon doors flew open and Loretta ran in.

"I'm gonna kill you!" Loretta said, pointing a shotgun of her own at Bumper, her hands trembling so bad she almost dropped it.

Bumper instantly drew and fired. She grabbed her chest and dropped the shotgun, staggering over a table and falling to the floor face-down, blood oozing out from underneath her.

"You're next, bitch," Bumper said as he turned toward Billie Jo with his gun in his hand.

She drew and put two bullets in his heart before he knew what happened. Blood ran down the front of his overalls as he dropped his gun and crashed to the floor like a big oak tree.

Billie Jo backed up to the bar, holding her Colt at the ready. Fuller had the hammers cocked and his fingers on the triggers of Big Boy as they both searched the saloon for more trouble, but it was all over. Digger checked Loretta for a heartbeat, then Bumper.

"They're both dead," he said.

Billie Jo holstered her Colt and Fuller eased the hammers down on Big Boy.

The card players laid their cards back on the tables. The piano player came back in and the drunks continued to drink. Except for Willie, he was passed out with his head on the table, his bottle empty. He never knew what happened.

"Thought he was going to kill you before I could kill him," Fuller said. "I forget how damn fast you are."

"I should have shot him when she ran in. I knew what he was going to do," Billie Jo said.

"Why did she do that? She didn't even know how to use a gun," Fuller said.

"Fear."

Homer Plat came in and saw Loretta and Bumper.

"Oh no," Homer said. "Bee said she saw Loretta run out with my shotgun."

"Take your gun and get out," Fuller said.

Homer picked up the shotgun, took a quick last look at Loretta and Bumper, and left.

Several people started crowding around the dead.

"Get away from them you ghouls," Fuller said. "Digger, take her body up to her room. Have her cleaned up. Find a woman to do it."

"What about Bumper?" Digger said.

"Don't know yet."

"I'll clean her up and find her a pretty dress," Billie Jo said. "My pa liked her and so did I after our talk."

A tall man picked up Bumper's gun, stuck it in his belt and prompted another man nearby to pick up Bumper by his feet. As they carried him toward the doors the tall man looked back toward Fuller and said, "He's our neighbor, we'll bury him."

Fuller nodded at them and then looked at Ernest.

"Get Shin to clean this mess up," Fuller said.

Ernest nodded and went through a door behind the bar.

Digger came walking down the stairs to Fuller.

"Billie Jo is taking care of her. What you want to do with her things?"

"She ain't got nobody. Give 'em to the church," Fuller said.

"They won't take them because of what she did for a living," Digger said.

"Burn them then," Fuller said. "I'll pay for the funeral."

"I'll dig the grave," Digger said.

Fuller got a fresh bottle of whiskey and poured a glass full. After he had about half the bottle drank, Billie Jo came down the stairs.

"I did the best I could for her. Need to get her a box. I wish you had shot him. That shotgun would have blown him in half."

"Wouldn't have made any difference to him," Fuller said. "When you're dead you're dead." He pulled his suspenders tighter.

"Men don't think a woman's life is worth as much as a man's," Billie Jo said. "Why White Hair murdered my mother."

"So that's the real reason you want to go to the Cheyenne. Not catchin' him has always been one of my biggest regrets. Somehow he out-rode us and got away. Didn't get close enough to make out what or who he was, except he had white hair and was wearing a Union Officer's uniform. Nobody was supposed to shoot women or children. Me and Lamont didn't show up in time to stop it."

"I'll never forget. If he's still alive I want to make sure he's not."

"It's likely too late," Fuller said. "What if I make you the new marshal? Would that change your mind and make you stay?"

"The marshal," Billie Jo repeated, grinning. "Don't think the town would let you do that. They wouldn't want a woman marshal."

"Wouldn't give them a choice," Fuller said. "I'm a federal judge, what I say goes."

"Nah, no can do," Billie Jo said. "Where's Slate and his men?"

"Rode over to Dodge to fetch some fresh horses. They're gonna move on pretty soon. It's getting bad up that way now. There's a war with the Indians, trying to drive them back to the reservations. Heard the Sioux and Cheyenne are getting together for a big battle with the army."

"When's Slate comin' back?"

"Tomorrow."

"Would you buy my place, Judge?"

"If it would keep you from riding that damn train."

"Can I trust Slate and his men?" Billie Jo asked.

"Think so," Fuller said. "But you shouldn't go. Known him for a few years. Ain't heard nothin' bad, but still thinking I might pay Digger to go along, too. He's getting restless here anyway. He's good with a rifle and you can trust him."

"You don't have to do that. I know you promised Pa to take care of me but it's time for me to move on."

"You're better off here."

"Not anymore."

"We'll talk more about this with them tomorrow," Fuller said.

"What about Loretta?"

"I'll get her a box and we'll close tomorrow in her honor."

"You have a soft spot I ain't seen before," Billie Jo said.

"Now keep that to yourself."

# 8

The next morning, Judge Fuller Newton was sitting at his table in the saloon, drinking coffee, painting a sign that read:

CLOSED TODAY FOR LORETTA

Ernest was lining up bottles on the shelf behind the bar and Willie was hugging a bottle of rotgut whiskey Digger had bought him.

The swinging doors swung open and Eddie the blacksmith came walking in.

"We're closed today but you can have some whiskey to take with you," Fuller said.

"Heard about you closing for Loretta," Eddie said.

"Yep."

"Why would you do that?"

"She worked here."

"I never heard of anyone closing for a whore."

"Well I am," Fuller said. "There's some good ninety-proof under the bar. Have a bottle on me."

"You bein' too friendly, Judge."

"No I'm not."

"Bullshit," Eddie said. "Out with it. What's buggin' you?"

"I need two horses shoed today. Make sure they're sound, that little mare Bittersweet you're boarding is a kicker. Don't know 'bout diggers horse. Billie Jo's going to Montana to the northern Cheyenne to find her family. Digger's goin' with her."

"Why is Digger goin'?" Eddie asked.

"'Cause I want him to."

"She needs a bigger horse to go that far. That mare ain't more than thirteen or fourteen hands high."

"Well she don't want one. Just get her horse shoed. She's got to get on with leaving the boarding house whatever she does."

"Why don't you let her stay here?"

"Men."

"That's goin' to happen wherever she is," Eddie said.

"Not here," Fuller said.

"She's going to need a lot of stuff on the trail, Judge. I got a damn good pack mule for a fair price."

Fuller wasn't paying attention, he had other thoughts on his mind.

"Told Billie Jo I would buy her place but I really don't need it," Fuller said. "It crossed my mind you might could make good use of the land. Think I'm goin' to have to go with her. Can't let her get killed. Promised I would take care of her. All you got is a livery stable and if you marry that pretty gal from Dodge you been courtin' she ain't gonna want to live in a livery stable."

"Knew you had something else up your sleeve," Eddie said.

"Would like you to take care of it for me while I'm gone?"

"How long you gonna be gone?"

"Don't know. I'll let you pay out twenty five acres to keep and then you can have the whole damn thing if me or Billie Jo don't make it back. You can marry that little gal and move in the house now."

"Well, would be better than what I got here," Eddie said. "You think Billie Jo will come back?"

"She don't know how bad things are out there," Fuller said. "She might."

"I'll do it," Eddie said.

"Good. I'll write you up a paper for four hundred dollars for the twenty-five acres, house and barn. Give me a hundred now to help with supplies then save ten a month for me. If we don't come back, the whole thing is yours for nothing."

"I can do that. Your word's good enough for me," Eddie said. He stuck out his big hand and shook hands with Judge Fuller.

"Keep this between you and me, though, for now," Fuller said. "And shoe them horses. I have to take care of her."

"Everybody knows what your real problem is, Judge. You're in love with Miss Billie Jo and she's not goin' to see it the way you do."

"Take your whiskey and go, Eddie," Fuller said. "Don't need any more trepidation."

"No never mind to me," Eddie said and walked out.

A few minutes later Digger came in. "I ran into Eddie on the street and he said I was goin' to Montana. That's the first I heard about it."

"I was goin' to talk to you about it," Fuller said. "Billie Jo needs someone she can trust to go along with her."

"I don't know, Judge, that's a long way from here and me and Billie Jo don't exactly get along."

"You'll be okay," Fuller said.

"What's goin' to happen to you, Judge? Everybody knows how you feel about her," Digger said. "Why don't you go?"

"I may have to, but I'm tired of hearing them pestiferous comments. And besides, what would I do with this damn place?"

"Sell it to Old Man Warren. He's been trying to buy it from you for years. Owns most of the town now and hired that gun hand Pervez to twist the arms of those who own the rest."

"Pervez is second rate. Billie Jo could take him," Fuller said. "Besides, I'm too old to start over."

"Slate's your age and he's still goin' strong."

"I'm too soft now, been taking it easy too long."

"You're just makin' excuses. You're afraid Billie Jo won't want you to go."

"She might not," Fuller said.

"I got eyes," Digger said. "She knows you love her and she loves you, but, like a papa."

"I don't know what to think," Fuller said.

"Tell you what, Judge—you go, I'll go. Betcha Warren still wants the saloon."

"You'll have to talk to Billie Jo for me, Digger."

"I will," Digger said.

"Put this sign out front for me and talk to her. I could take 'no' a lot easier from you."

"I think you should start packing," Digger said.

# 9

After Digger hung the sign up and headed for the boarding house, Judge Fuller was sitting by himself, sipping whiskey and thinking about selling the place. A little bit into his thinking and sipping, Slate showed up with Glover and Hatchet.

"Saw your sign, Judge," Slate said. "Why are you closed for Loretta?"

"Bumper killed her and then Billie Jo killed him yesterday. Was a nasty day. Glad you're back."

"We found some work with the army out of Fort Dodge," Slate said. "We start next week as scouts. They're going to send Company C up to Rosebud, Montana to chase some Indians back to the reservation. The pay's too good to turn down. I think I can get them to let Billie Jo tag along with us if she will do what they say. We'll keep an eye on her. You put your money back in your pocket."

"She don't like the army," Fuller said. "They murdered her mama when she was little. She remembers it all, too. Me and her pa were in the outfit that did it. Nobody was supposed to kill women and children. Lamont didn't know they were in that village until it was all over. Not sure she'd have anything to do with the army now. Decided I was gonna sell the saloon to that carpet bagger Warren and go with Billie Jo and Digger."

"If you go when the army goes you'll be better off," Slate said. "You're all tough as hickory nuts, but even better with the army not too far away."

"I guess I got to do it," Fuller said.

"Looks like you do. Sorry to hear about Loretta," Slate said.

"Ya'll go ahead and get a bottle and we'll have a goodbye drink," Fuller said, motioning to Slate and his men.

"Thanks, we'll take you up on that," Hatchet said. He went behind the bar and got a bottle and four glasses and they sat down with the Judge.

"Here's to Loretta," Slate said and everyone raised their glass and drank.

"What made you decide to go, Judge, you rule us out?" Glover said and poured himself another drink.

"No, you boys are good. I just realized how damn lonesome I would be. Been helping raise that kid since she was six."

Hatchet had already abandoned the glass and was drinking straight from the bottle.

"Slow down, Hatchet," Slate said. "We got to get supplies and I'm goin' to need your help."

"I be alright. Thanks for the whiskey, Judge," Hatchet said and grabbed the bottle. "I'll take this with me. How much?"

"On me, Hatchet, hope you find Crooked Leg," Fuller said.

"I will," Hatchet said. "Heard that bastard was on the trail, a place called Little Big Horn. I'm goin' to quarter him real slow."

The doors opened and Billie Jo and Digger walked in.

"Hello guys," Billie Jo said.

"Howdy," Slate said and the other two nodded.

"Digger told me you're goin' with us, Judge," Billie Jo said. "I was hoping you would."

"There's been a change of plans all the way around," Fuller said. "Slate and the boys have joined the army for a while, as scouts goin' to Montana. Thinks you can go with them and the army up to Cheyenne country if you want."

"Don't think so," Billie Jo said. "Too many bad memories of the army. Don't want to go on the train either. Guess it's just the three of us."

"What we figured," Slate said. "We'll probably see you on the trail." He turned to Fuller. "What about being a judge?"

"Goin' to hang on to the title for now," Fuller said. "Might need it to get out of a jam."

"Good, we might need you," Slate said. "Goodbye and good luck. Never know until it happens. Always ready to help you if I can."

"Same goes for us," Fuller said.

# 10

It was an hour past the time Old Man Warren agreed to meet to buy the saloon. Fuller was sitting at his favorite table drinking coffee with Digger, who had a glass of sarsaparilla, and Big Boy beside them on the table. It was raining and thundering so hard it sounded like a brigade of soldiers marching across the sky.

"I wonder if Warren has chickened out?" Fuller said. He drank the last drop of coffee and then picked up the whiskey bottle and poured a shot glass full and sipped. "I done bought all the supplies, even Eddie's mule, but it'll all be for nothing if Warren don't buy the damn place."

"Probably just the rain slowin' him down. He'll show," Digger said.

The doors swung open and Ozzie Warren walked in with an umbrella over his New York bolero hat and a slicker on. He took a couple of steps inside and stopped just out of the reach of the rain from the swinging doors, folded the umbrella and took off the slicker and dropped them against the wall.

Warren's gunslinger Pervez came in behind him. He kept his hat and slicker on and let the water drip and run across the floor. He stood next to Warren's umbrella and slicker with his hand on his pearl-handled Colt, his beady brown eyes staring at Fuller. His holster was tied down and cut away to make it a fast-draw rig. His black hat had a rattlesnake band on it, covering his dirty black hair. He had a dark complexion and was of average height. Warren made sure everyone knew Pervez's reputation as a killer to frighten people into doing what he wanted them to do.

"Sorry we're late," Warren said. "Got a frog-strangler goin' on out there."

He walked over to Fuller's table holding his hat and hung it on the rack on the wall as water dripped off the brim. Pervez stayed put, leaning against the wall.

Warren was getting up in years but still trim for an old man with wavy gray hair. He was wearing a nice black suit with a gold watch chain hanging from his vest pocket to his pants pocket.

"Have a seat, Warren," Fuller said and pushed Big Boy over on the table.

Warren was eyeing the eight-gauge as he sat down. "Nasty this morning," he said, "but we have business to conduct."

"Would you like a drink, Mr. Warren?" Digger asked.

"No, boy, don't have time. You sign the contract, Judge?"

"I did." Fuller reached in his coat and laid the contract on the table. Warren pulled a check out of his vest pocket and laid it on the table. Fuller picked it up, looked at it and put it in his coat pocket. Warren picked up the contract and put it in his pocket.

"Any other family members I have to deal with for the ownership of this place you haven't told me 'bout, Judge?"

"No, I'm it," Fuller said. "All my folks and my wife died by Indian hands."

"Okay then, the deal is done," Warren said. "Gonna have to clean this place up some. Get rid of that rundown bar and the stained mirror. Maybe paint it to hide the dirt. The sooner you can get out the better."

"I don't give a damn what you do," Fuller said. "Leaving today. You did say you would keep my help working for you?"

"We agreed orally on that but we didn't set a salary or a length of employment. That about right?" Warren said.

"Yes," Fuller said.

"Then I can pay who I want to work and fire them as I please. There's nothin' written in the contract."

"You know, you are a son of a bitch," Fuller said.

"I will retain the piano player," Warren said. "Ernest and the flatheads can work for the rest of the week before I will fire them. I have four young ladies on their way here to make this a real saloon. Now get out."

Pervez straightened up from the wall, grinning.

Fuller moved his hand past Big Boy, picked a bottle of whiskey off the table and handed it to Digger.

"Hold on to this, Digger, while I say my goodbyes."

"That's not yours anymore," Warren said. "You have to pay for the whiskey you drink in here now, Judge."

Pervez stepped out on the floor next to Warren.

"Pay him," Pervez said and placed his hand on his Colt handle.

Fuller locked eyes with Pervez.

"You really think you can tell me what to do, snake shit," Fuller said.

Pervez gripped his Colt and Fuller jumped up, whirling around like a streak of lightning and kicking Pervez in the balls. He dropped his hand from the Colt and Fuller grabbed Big Boy from the table and smashed Pervez's nose with the butt of the shotgun and drew the Colt from his holster as he fell to the floor, blood running from his nose and mouth.

Fuller tossed the shotgun to Digger and stuck Pervez's Colt in his belt.

"Watch him, Digger," he said, nodding toward Pervez and kicked a startled Warren's chair out from under him.

Fuller snatched Warren up by the collar and grabbed him by the seat of the pants and threw him out the doors into the muddy street. He fell on all fours, his gold chain and watch dropping in the mud, his nice black suit now wet and muddy.

Digger carried Big Boy and the bottle of whiskey out into the rain.

"Don't have to worry about Pervez, Judge, he's out cold, bleedin' like a stuck hog. He may never have a nose again."

Fuller kicked Warren, scooped up a handful of mud and rubbed it on the old man's face. Several people were standing in the rain, watching and laughing. Warren staggered to his feet, wiping mud from his face. He left his watch in the mud and ran back in the saloon. Fuller pulled Pervez's Colt out of his belt and dropped it in the mud, disappearing under the muck.

"You're still hell on wheels," Digger said and handed Fuller the shotgun. He held up the whiskey bottle. "Think we might have that drink now."

"Later," Fuller said. "Go get Billie Jo. I'll get to the bank and meet you at Eddie's. Hope we don't regret going to Cheyenne country."

"It was your idea for me to come along, if you remember."

"Well it was your idea for me to go, Digger."

"You have a better reason to go," Digger said. "Billie Jo don't cotton to me much."

"We done made a commitment. A man never knows what's being done to him when a woman's doing it. Go get her."

Lightning flashed across the sky and a clap of thunder scared the hell out of two horses left out in the rain. They jerked loose from the hitching post and people were running for cover. The wind picked up and blew the rain across the muddy street toward them, slapping them in the face as they ran.

"Okay, I'm goin'," Digger said, pulling his hat down tighter.

"Good, meet you at Eddie's," Fuller said, wiping the rain from his face.

By the time Digger got to the boarding house the rain showed no sign of slowing down. He and Billie Jo hugged the side of buildings to shield themselves from the rain as they walked to Eddie's. No sign of Warren or Pervez. The Judge showed up with the money from the bank and Eddie fixed vittles for them as they all dried out.

"Thanks for the grub, Eddie," Fuller said. He stepped closer to Eddie and in a whisper he said, "Marry that gal already, and take care of her."

"I will, Judge," Eddie said.

"Okay, let's saddle up," Fuller said in a firmer voice. "I'm going to give the orders unless you think one of you has more experience?"

They both shook their head no.

"Digger, you take the lead. Billie Jo, you're in the middle. And I'll pull up the drag with the mule. That okay with everyone?"

Digger and Billie Jo nodded again.

"Might be a good time to leave before Warren finds him some more help," Fuller said. He stuck his Winchester in the saddle scabbard and hung Big Boy on the saddle horn.

"Digger told me what happened," Billie Jo said, looking at the Judge. "Wish I could have seen that. We better get out of town before he comes after us. Don't want to have to kill him."

"Yeah let's haul ass, we'll hold up at the stage station near Winston for the night," Fuller said.

They all climbed up in their saddle.

"So long, Eddie," Digger said. "Watch out for Warren."

"I will," Eddie said.

"I'll be in touch," Fuller said.

Eddie nodded.

"Bye and thanks," Billie Jo said.

"Good luck," Eddie said as the others started their ride out of town.

# 11

The rain moved on to the west and left behind wet prairie ground that kept the dust down and made the ride to the Wells Fargo stage station on the edge of Winston less tormenting from heat and dust.

The stage station was the last white man's place for fifty miles. It was a dug-in—about three feet in the ground to keep it from blowing away with the strong prairie winds—a home for the stage manager and a place for passengers to rest while their horses were being changed.

The station manager came out of the stables and saw the three coming. He waited for them to ride up. He had been there since the war and looked it. He was pot-bellied with whiskers down to his chest, wearing a faded blue shirt and his old Union army pants. The pistol he was carrying was a Remington army issue.

"Howdy, Judge, thought that was you," the manager said. "You got another back shooter?"

"No, we're riding through on our way to Montana," Judge Fuller said.

"That's a long way from here. Got a stage next week you could ride, just two changes all the way there."

Digger and Billie Jo didn't say anything.

"We want to keep these horses and that makes things complicated," Fuller said.

"Yeah, I guess so," the station manager said. "I can see why you would want that little mare. Pretty thing. Only trouble is the Indians will, too. They would kill you for a horse with those kind of markings. Think she was a gift from the great spirit or something."

Fuller turned to introduce the others. "This is Digger and Billie Jo, the marshal's daughter." He turned back straight in his saddle and motioned toward the man in front of them. "This is Charlie Evans, he runs the place."

"Glad to meet you," Charlie said to Digger and then turned to Billie Jo, taking off his hat and holding it against his chest. "Heard what happened to your pa, ma'am. He was a good man."

"Thank you," Billie Jo said.

Digger shook his head in agreement as Charlie placed his hat back on his head.

"Charlie, can we pay you for some grub and feed for the horses," Fuller said. "Maybe a room for the night? Got a long ride 'fore we get to civilization again after we leave here."

"No charge for your food, but have to charge fifty cents apiece for your horses eating company feed. No beds available tonight but you can sleep on your saddles inside."

"Sounds good enough to me," Fuller said.

Digger and Billie Jo agreed.

"Put your horses in the stables," Charlie said. "Go ahead and feed them, too, I'll tell my wife to cook you up something for supper."

"Thank you," Fuller said.

They rode their horses into the stable and dismounted, scaring the other horses into the end of the stable. Digger and Billie Jo pulled their rifles from the scabbards; Fuller, his shotgun strap off the saddle horn and the Winchester from the scabbard.

"We better enjoy this supper," Fuller said. "It's going to be a while 'fore we get another hot meal and a roof over our head. It's a long ride from here."

They nodded and unsaddled their horses. Fuller unsaddled the Appaloosa and lead him and the mule to the water trough.

As they neared the station, toting their saddles and weapons, a two-horse wagon appeared on the trail at the top of a hill about a half-mile away, coming toward the stage station. Charlie stepped out of the building and walked up to the others.

"Know who that is, Charlie?" Fuller asked.

"Nope. Can't tell from here," Charlie said. "Might better wait and find out his intent. Been havin' a lot of strange ones ride by lately. Most just hungry, though."

As the wagon got closer, a man wearing tattered old dirty clothes and a Union army cap was reining the wagon. He looked like he was old enough to have fought in the war and hadn't taken a bath since.

"I can make him out now," Charlie said. "Comes by two or three times a year, name's Rufus Magee. Smells like a gutted hog all the time. Peddles whores. Oh sorry, ma'am, forgot you was here."

Billie didn't say anything.

The wagon rolled up close enough for them to see four pretty young women in the wagon. All the women had their hands bound. One was wearing a traditional Chinese silk shirt and pants and a bamboo hat. None of the girls could be older than eighteen, Fuller thought.

Rufus stopped the wagon at the stable entrance, picked his Spencer up from the seat and climbed down and walked up to Charlie, who backed off from the smell.

"Need to feed my girls and horses," Rufus said.

"Why do you have them girls tied?" Billie Jo asked.

He looked at Billie Jo, squelched one eye. "So nobody can steal them. What you want to know fer?"

"Turn them loose, mister," Billie Jo said.

"Mind your own business, they my property."

Fuller pointed Big Boy at the man.

"Mr. Magee, my name is Fuller Newton. I'm a federal judge and it's very plain what you're doing. Can't let you sell them women. Cut 'em loose."

"None of the lawmen care 'round here," Rufus said. "They tied for protection. They going willingly."

"Bullshit," Fuller said.

Digger was holding his Winchester on the old man, and Billie Jo her Colt.

"Whores belong to whoever buys them," Rufus said.

"What you think we had a war for," Fuller said. "Looks like you were in it."

"Was," Rufus said. "At Gettysburg."

"Me too," Charlie said.

"Looks like we all was there," Fuller said.

"I paid fifty dollars apiece for them whores. They come in all the way from San Francisco," Rufus said. "That's a lot of money. They my property."

"How much do you sell them for?" Fuller said.

"Two hundred each," he said and grinned. "Already sold 'em all to a man named Warren down at the Gallop Saloon in Rainbow Peak. He'll make thousands off these girls."

"Not now he won't," Fuller said. "Don't have time to take you to jail but the next best thing is to give them your wagon and let them go."

"Give them my wagon! You got no right to do that," Rufus said.

"I'm making one," Fuller said and waved the barrel of Big Boy at Rufus.

"Judge, that's not right," Charlie said and pulled out his gun. "I think you oughta let Magee keep what's his."

"Can't do that, Charlie," Fuller said. "Drop the guns, you two. Don't do nothin' foolish or this shotgun will blow both of you apart with one blast. Billie Jo, you and Digger cut 'em loose."

The four women never moved after they had been cut loose, just sat there.

"What the hell's wrong with you ladies, you're free," Fuller said. "Take the wagon and go."

All of them stared at the Judge with a blank look except the girl in the bamboo hat. She looked to be the youngest.

"We go with dirty man," she said. The other girls nodded.

"You don't want to leave on your own?" Fuller said.

"They been threatened so much they don't know what to say," Billie Jo said.

"No, she just knows she's got a money maker," Rufus said.

"Shut up, Magee," Fuller said.

"This is all we know," the young girl said.

Fuller sat on his saddle for a few moments, thinking about the situation.

"Okay, Rufus, get the hell out of here," Fuller said.

"And my girls?" Rufus said.

Fuller nodded.

"You can't let him do that," Billie Jo said.

"That's just wrong, Judge," Digger said.

"They're going with him willingly. I got no grounds to charge him on," Fuller said. "We got to move on."

Rufus, not wanting to press his luck, picked up his rifle and headed on towards Rainbow Peak.

Charlie told the other three to join him for supper later and went back in the station.

Digger and Billie Jo didn't say anything.

"Well, what is it?" Fuller said.

"Not my place to say," Digger said.

Billie Jo stared at the Judge and opened her mouth to say something, but closed it instead, then walked off in silence.

# 12

They rode out of the stable at the crack of dawn the next morning. The tension in the air had mostly settled.

"Digger, you check the goat bags?" Judge Fuller said.

"Yeah, they're full," Digger said.

"Good. We have to get across the open prairie without being ambushed by bucks. They run you down out there, torture you to death and take what you have. It's a hard day's ride to the mountains from here. We'll walk the horses for now, save them to outrun and outlast the Indians if they show up. Let's get on with it."

By noon the ground began to dry out from the sun and the dust picked up, blowing a dust curtain across the prairie. They each tied a bandana over their face and shirts over the horses' eyes and trudged on for most of the day, their horses in a walk. A turn of the wind cleared the dust in late afternoon and they got rid of the extra layers and rode on for the next ten miles. A stench floated in on the wind and they spotted buzzards circling in the distance.

"The smell of death," Digger said. "Know it well."

"Be ready to run," Fuller said. "I'll have to leave the mule if we do."

As they approached, the buzzards scattered from two dead horses and two naked dead men. The horses were full of arrows and bullet holes, with intestines hanging from their open guts, eyes plucked out. The men were mutilated. Clothes scattered nearby. Arrows stuck in their ears, their eyes also gone. Their genitals had been stuffed in their mouths, heads scalped.

Fuller dismounted, hanging on to the mule rope, picked up an arrow and looked at it. "Sioux." He did a complete turn, eyeing the surroundings. "Don't see nothin' out there now." He grabbed the arm of one of the dead men.

Billie Jo sat on her horse, throwing up.

"He ain't stiff yet," Fuller said. "Ain't been long since this was done. Let's get the hell out of here. The mountain is close enough now we can make a run for it."

Fuller mounted the Appaloosa and tugged on the mule to get him started. Billie Jo and Digger took off, spurring their horses to a full gallop. They rode hard until they reached the foot of the mountain, Fuller bringing up the drag with the mule. They kept walking the horses and mule through the trees to let them have a slow, cooling breather before stopping to rest.

"Them Sioux may have seen us coming," Fuller said. "Need to find a place with some rocks against our backs and be ready for hostiles."

"There's a crevasse over there," Digger said, pointing at it.

"Let's go," Fuller said, pulling on the mule rope.

They rode the horses into the crevasse, tied the animals to a scrub bush and took positions to watch their surroundings. A few minutes later, they heard branches snapping to their front and spotted two painted Indian ponies walking through the thick trees toward them with no riders. The ponies kept coming their way with no sign of any riders and eventually stopped in a small clearing and started nibbling grass.

"Where the hell are the riders," Digger said.

"They're out there somewhere," Fuller said.

Out of nowhere, blood-curling screams came bouncing off the rocks from behind them and two bucks jumped from the rocks into the crevasse, one knocking Digger down and the other one landing next to Billie Jo with a knife in his hand. She stepped back, drew her Colt and put two quick bullets in the man. He dropped the knife, staggered toward her and fell dead at her feet. Digger was wrestling with the other buck, managed to kick him away as Fuller stuck the eight-gauge to the side of his head and pulled both triggers, blood and brain-matter splattering on Billie Jo and Digger. The remaining stump that once was the man's head rolled to a stop a few feet away. The painted ponies took off running from the sound of the shotgun blast. Digger grabbed the reins of their horses to keep them from running, too.

"Holy shit," Digger said. "I got Indian all over me."

"Me too," Billie Jo said.

"You can rinse off but don't use too much of our water," Fuller said.

Digger and Billie Jo poured water on a bandana and washed up the best they could.

"We got to find a creek, Judge," Billie Jo said.

"When we come to one. Be glad you're alive."

"I am, but I got to get this off me. It's givin' me the willies."

"Me too," Digger said.

Fuller nodded and walked over to his Appaloosa, climbed on and hung Big Boy on the saddle horn. "Let's get to some higher ground," he said.

They followed a winding overgrown trail up the mountain until they saw an old abandon shack and mine shaft with bushes growing in front of the mine entrance.

"Look," Digger said, pointing.

"A place to hold up for awhile," Billie Jo said.

"We have to move on," Fuller said. "We'll divide up the stuff among us and leave the mule with what we can't carry as a peace offering."

"You leavin' whiskey?" Digger said.

"Brought that to use for trade when we need it," Fuller said. "Put some bottles in your saddle bags. Warren would pee his pants if he knew I carried out two cases of his best whiskey."

"Four bottles do it?" Digger said.

"Should be enough," Fuller said. "Billie Jo, give the horses some water and grain. Me and Digger will load what we can carry on our horses and get on down the trail 'fore them Indians find us."

No more than two miles after they left the mine, they saw flames flickering through the trees and smelled a wind-blown meat smell drifting overhead.

"That smell is makin' me hungry," Digger said.

"That's the mule," Fuller said.

"Guess I'm not that hungry."

The Judge grinned. "May come a day when you will."

They let their horses have their head in a walk through the thick trees and brush as a half-moon moved across the sky to take its place when the fading sun dropped off the mountain.

"We gonna ride in the dark, Judge?" Digger said.

"We'll hold up for the night and hope the Sioux do too. They don't like to fight at night for fear of losin' their spirit but will if they're after something bad enough. Just hope what they're after isn't us."

They dismounted and walked their horses to a rock overhang, tied them to a nearby tree limb and left them saddled in case they were forced to ride in the dark. The half-moon was in its place now for the night and they were in the only place they could be. Fuller passed out some hardtack and they frowned when he handed it to them.

"Can't start no fire. That's it for tonight," Fuller said.

"Billie Jo, you still think you want to go to the Cheyenne?" Digger said.

"Right now I just want to find a creek, wash this smell off me."

"We'll hunker down here and move out in the morning," Fuller said. "Should be a creek on the other side of the mountain. Ya'll catch a wink. I'll keep watch 'til I tire out and wake one of you up for your turn."

"I know who that will be," Digger said.

"Go lay down," Fuller said.

They took their bed rolls off their horses. Fuller sat down with Big Boy, pushed himself up against a rock, stretched his legs out and crossed them. Digger and Billie Jo dozed off a little later on their bed rolls.

Not long after Billie Jo went to sleep, Fuller noticed she was pulling her body into a fetal position, sobbing quietly in her sleep. He got up and walked over to her and shook her. She woke up, grabbed her Colt and cocked it before he could speak.

"Whoa, Billie Jo, it's me," Fuller said, grabbing the barrel of the Colt. "You were having a nightmare."

He let go of the gun and Billie Jo relaxed her arm and sighed.

"I'm awake now, thanks." She wiped sweat from her face and put her Colt back in the holster. "Been havin' the same nightmare all my life."

"I know," Fuller said.

"What happened," Digger asked.

"The monster, White Hair. My Cheyenne mother was murdered at Sand Creek when I was eight. We ran for the river and a soldier kept coming at us, waving his sword. He had long white hair flowing from a blue cavalry hat and was riding a big black horse. He swung his sword as he went by, driving it through my mother, and kept going, leaving the sword in her as he disappeared over a hill."

"Maybe he's still in Cheyenne country," Digger said.

"You got a real name?" Billie Jo said. "Digger's kind of spooky."

"Digger's alright with me, but if you have to know, it's Eli Rose."

"What about you, Billie Jo?" Digger said. "I'm guessing that's not your Cheyenne name."

"Broken Moon," she said. "My pa said the first thing they saw when I was born was clouds drifting across a full moon. He said it looked like it had been broken into pieces, so that's what they named me. Had a brother named Two Moons. Me and some other kids hid in the grass along the river bank during the attack, but I never did see my brother again."

"If White Hair is out here anywhere we'll find him," Fuller said.

Billie Jo instinctively placed her hand on the barrel of her Colt.

"I'm goin' to find him if he's still alive," she said. "And if he is, I'll make sure he won't be much longer."

# 13

By the time the sun winked at daylight they were riding.

The morning air was crisp. A haze floated through the tall pines, the snow melting into a soft pad as the horses high-stepped through the mix of mud and snow pervading the pure air out of their nostrils like a steam locomotive.

"It's May and it's still cold," Digger said. "Don't it ever warm up?"

"Gets down to around thirty or so at night in the summer up here," Judge Fuller said. "We get off this mountain it'll warm up. Hell, it'll get downright hot."

"I got to get this smell off me, cold or not. Changing clothes didn't do much good," Billie Jo said.

"It's been two days now," Digger said. "I got used to it."

"That's disgusting," Billie Jo said. "You been around the dead too much."

"Death is a way of life in Cheyenne country," Fuller said. "That's the main reason I didn't want you to come out here. You're not gonna like what you see."

"All I see now is pine trees and snow," Billie Jo said. "You know how long it will take us to get to civilization again?"

"Used to be a stage coach rest stop 'bout half a day's ride from here called Hell's Rock, unless them Indians got to it already," Fuller said.

"They still after us, you think?" Digger said.

"No sign of them but you never know. In my experience, they can be your friend, though, if you've got something for them. That's why we brought the whiskey."

Another mile down the road, Billie Jo jumped off Bittersweet and began unbuckling her gun belt.

"You two turn your horses the other way so I can pee." She dropped her pants and squatted behind a fallen oak tree nearby.

With his back turned to Billie Jo, Digger hear a sound like a buzzing bumble bee whizzing through the air and suddenly an arrow pinned his hat to a pine tree inches from his head.

Three Sioux riders appeared, charging toward them from the trees.

Digger jerked the reins tight on his horse and wheeled around, fumbling for his Winchester in the scabbard. Fuller grabbed Big Boy off the saddle horn and took aim at the lead rider, no more than twenty yards away, and blasted him off his pony. The animal kept running on down the trail.

The other two riders were headed for Billie Jo.

Billie Jo pulled her pants up in a frenzy and snatched the Colt out of the holster on the ground. She jumped on the fallen tree and hurled herself on the pony behind the rider and fired a bullet into his brain, a shower of blood soaking her and the pony.

The dead man fell off as the last rider grabbed hold of Bittersweet's reins and took off, leading her in a run on his pony.

Billie Jo stuck the Colt in her pants and rode by Digger on the pony, grabbing his Winchester and chasing them up a hill. She stopped, aimed the Winchester and fired. The rider dropped Bittersweet's reins and fell off his pony. She rode up to Bittersweet, leaped off the pony and put another round in the fallen rider out of anger.

Fuller rode up beside her, shaking his head. "You're something else, gal."

Digger pulled up next to her. He had his hat on with a jagged hole in it.

"Here's your rifle back," she said and pitched it to him.

"That horse of yours is going to cause a lot of problems with the Indians," Fuller said. "Those pretty markings might as well be a target."

"Maybe you oughta help a little more next time," Billie Jo said.

"Maybe you oughta get rid of her," Fuller said.

"No way," Billie Jo said.

"It would help if we could get out of this pine thicket," Digger said.

"Got to go get my gun belt and finish what I started," Billie Jo said.

Fuller and Digger grinned. Billie Jo didn't think it was amusing and rode away.

"Go on, I'll catch up," she yelled and kept going.

"We'll give her a few minutes and wait here," Fuller said.

Billie Jo rode back to the fallen oak, dismounted and picked up her gun belt. She looked around but before she could lower her pants she heard the brush rattling behind her.

A grizzly bear came running out of the bushes toward her, stopped, reared up on his hind legs and growled. She screamed and Bittersweet jerked the reins out of her hand and took off running from the bear.

"You hear that?" Digger said.

"Yeah," Fuller said.

They turned around and spurred their horses and saw Bittersweet galloping toward them. Fuller snatched Big Boy off the saddle horn. Billie Jo came into view, running down the trail on foot with her Colt in one hand the gun belt in the other, the grizzly gaining on her.

Fuller rode up to her and held his hand out. Billie Jo stuck the Colt in her pants as she was pulled up on the back of Fuller's appaloosa. He raised the shotgun barrel in the air, cocked it and pulled a trigger. The blast scared the bear and he ran off in the pines.

Digger came riding up with Bittersweet.

"Why didn't you shoot that bear?" Digger said, staring at Billie Jo.

"We're in his territory," Fuller said.

"Yeah, that's why I didn't try to kill him, either," Billie Jo said.

"Looks like you can't drop your britches around here," Digger said and smiled.

She jerked Bittersweet's reins away from Digger and mounted the horse. "Let's get the hell out of here." She clucked at Bittersweet and galloped away.

Digger and Fuller looked at each other shrugged their shoulders. It was all they could do to keep from laughing as she rode out ahead of them.

Further down the mountain, Billie Jo stopped on a bluff, looking at a train rolling down the tracks at the foot of the mountain. It was slowing down at a water tower next to a small crew shack. The other two caught up to Billie Jo and stopped beside her.

"That the bad train you been telling us about," Digger said.

"That's the one, Western Yellowstone. An old steam engine," Fuller said. "Ain't no law out here, only the Indians and the soldiers killing each other. Neither one cares what the cutthroats are doing. A bunch show up every year about this time to rustle cattle that got lost during the winter and pick up women for the ride, whether they want to go or not."

"Where's that station at," Billie Jo said.

"It's on over that next hill, about three miles off the tracks," Fuller said.

The train stopped beside the water tower and a man climbed up the ladder to swing the water arm around to the engine tank.

"Let's stay here until they move on," Fuller said.

The sliding doors to two cars were slid open by a man wearing striped overalls and a railroad cap. Several cowboys jumped to the ground on foot and walked around.

A body was tossed out of one of the cars and hit the ground. It looked like an Indian woman wearing a buckskin top, naked from the waist down.

A few minutes later, a horse ramp slid out of a car to the ground and two cowboys rode out. One on a buckskin holding a young pretty Cheyenne woman across his horse's neck, the other one on a bay. When they cleared the ramp to the ground the one on the buckskin pushed the woman off the horse and picked her up by a rope he had around her neck and led her to the crew shack. They dismounted and tied their horses to a hitching post.

Both looked like young saddle bums with long hair and beards and dirty old sheepskin coats. The one on the buckskin was much bigger than the other one, with broad shoulders and a Colt slung low like he knew how to use it. The other one had a Colt stuck in his belt. They both had rifles on their saddles. They went in the shack, the big one leading the woman inside.

The man in the overalls picked up the leather strap on the water arm, climbed the ladder back up the tower and tied the water arm back to the tank. The train let out billowing black smoke and blew the whistle. All the cowboys on the ground boarded the train cars. The railroad man on the ground closed the car doors and climbed back on the engine, leaving the ones with the horses in the crew shack.

The engine started huffing and puffing and blew the whistle again. The two cowboys' horses started dancing frantically around the hitching post, throwing their heads up and down.

The train picked up speed and blew the whistle once more. The horses spun around the hitching post several times, breaking loose and galloping off for parts unknown.

The two cowboys ran out of the crew shack yelling for their horses to come back but they kept running until they disappeared over a nearby hill. The big cowboy took off his hat and slammed it to the ground.

"Son of a bitch!" he said so loud they could hear him from their hiding place in the trees. He jerked the woman down with the rope and kicked her in anger.

"What now?" Digger said.

"We'll go get the Cheyenne." Billie Jo rode out of the trees toward the tracks.

"Digger, you hold back and stay out of sight," Fuller said. "Keep your Winchester ready. If they draw on us, shoot 'em."

Billie Jo and the Judge rode to the tracks and crossed over to where the cowboys were standing.

"Howdy," the big one said. "Looks like we afoot now. Horses ran off. Name's Row. This here's Hollis. Could we double up with you to ride to the station? The squaw can walk."

"Why did you get off the train?" Fuller said.

"Headed to the Hell Rock stage station," Row said. "Gonna trade our horses for a ticket to California."

"But the train don't go that far," Hollis said.

"Why you goin' to California," Fuller said.

"That's where we can find gold," Row said. "Now it looks like they gonna go without us." He grinned and tugged on the rope around the woman's neck, jerking her down. "I'd trade ya the squaw for a horse."

"Turn her loose," Billie Jo said.

"She belongs to me," Row said.

"You're gonna walk and you're gonna turn her loose," Fuller said. He grabbed Big Boy off the saddle and leveled it on the men. "Drop your guns on the ground."

The cowboys complied and let their weapons drop.

"Do you understand me," Fuller said, looking at the Cheyenne woman. "Do you know that dead woman they threw off the train?"

"No," she said. "Already on train."

"What do they call you," Fuller said.

"Star Morning." She looked at Billie Jo. "What they call you?"

"Billie Jo, but my Cheyenne name is Broken Moon. My mother was murdered at Sand Creek twelve years ago."

"Two Moon family?"

"Yes, my brother is Half Moon. Do you know where he is?"

"With Sitting Bull."

"Take the rope off her," Billie Jo said.

Row put his hand on his Colt handle.

"You go for that gun, I'll cut you in half," Fuller said.

"How come you're with them?" Billie Jo asked.

"Killed my mother and brother when we sleep. Take me on train and have way with me."

"Come on now," Row said. "You gonna believe that? Make your squaw shut up and help us out."

"I was just asking the good Lord if he would hold it against me if I killed you," Fuller said.

"You wouldn't shoot a couple of unarmed men, would you," Hollis said.

"I might," Fuller said. "Now take the rope off her."

Row slipped the rope over her head and she moved over beside Billie Jo.

Fuller turned his appaloosa toward Digger and waved for him to come out. A few minutes later, Digger rode out into the open and down the hill to the railroad tracks.

"Was you gonna ambush us?" Hollis said.

"Considered it," Fuller said.

Star Morning grabbed the Winchester out of Billie Jo's saddle scabbard and started pumping bullets into Row and Hollis as fast as she could cock the rifle. They jumped around like popcorn, twisting and turning as the bullets hit them. Hollis gasped and fell on his knees, then to the ground, dead. Row staggered away and Star Morning put two more bullets in him before he hit the ground and rolled over on his back, still breathing. She dropped the Winchester, walked up to him and spit on him. He blinked his foggy brown eyes then closed them forever. She unbuckled his gun belt and spun him over, pulling it off and leaving him face down. Then she picked up the two Colts, strapped Row's on and stuck Hollis's in her belt.

Billie Jo rode up to her and reached out a hand. Star Morning picked up the Winchester and stuck it in the scabbard, took Billie Jo's hand and climbed up on Bittersweet.

"She made quick work of them," Digger said. "I'm not buryin' them."

"Just the girl," Fuller said. "I'll help you."

Digger and Fuller dug a grave, buried the Cheyenne girl and rode away with Billie Jo and Star Morning.

Along the way to the stage station, they spotted the cowboys' horses nibbling on a rich patch of grass. With no distractions, they rode up beside them and picked up the reins.

"Your bounty, Star Morning, you want them?" Fuller asked.

She nodded her head. "Yes, I go back to Rosebud."

She mounted the buckskin and lead the bay to the top of a ridge, then waved and disappeared to the other side.

"The station's just over that hill," Fuller said.

"Good," Billie Jo said. "We can finally get a bath."

# 14

Smoke curled out of the cabin chimney toward the mountains. Digger and Fuller sat at a table drinking whiskey from bottles, water heating on a stove so Billie Jo could take a bath. Inside the small log cabin were four tables, a wood-burning stove and a bar with a few pots and pans hanging on the wall. A lean-to was attached out the back door where they could bathe, and a privy with a half-moon carved out of the door stood some twenty paces away down a beaten path.

A stage pulled up. From inside the cabin they could hear the stage manager and driver talking about changing horses.

A tall well-dressed gentleman walked in the front door. He had long brown hair flowing from under a wide-brim hat, a thick mustache covering his upper lip, and was wearing a buckskin shirt with rawhide pants and knee-high black boots. Two pearl-handled Colts were in the front of his belt in a cross draw position. He took off his hat and walked over to a table on the other side of the room, dropped his hat on the table, pulled out a chair and sat down with his back to the wall, giving Digger and Fuller the once-over with his dark brown eyes.

Digger and Fuller gave him a glance and went back to drinking whiskey.

The man pointed a finger at a glass on the table and placed a coin beside the glass. One of the saloon girls saw him and brought a bottle of whiskey to the table and poured the glass full. He picked up the glass and downed the whiskey in one gulp. After wiping his mouth, he turned the glass upside-down and slid it out on the table to indicate that was all he wanted.

The door to the lean-to rattled open and a different saloon girl came in and motioned for Billie Jo to take her bath. The men kept drinking whiskey without talking. About thirty minutes later, Billie Jo opened the lean-to door and walked into the room fully dressed, her Colt on her hip, a towel in her hand. She sat down at the table and continued drying her long black hair.

"Okay, you two, get in there and get your bath," she said. "I already paid for it. Plus, I can't stand to be around either of you any longer without one," Billie Jo said.

Fuller and Digger looked at each for help but neither spoke. They put the corks back in their bottles, stood up and disappeared through the door.

Billie Jo looked at the man sitting on the other side of the room. He had a smile on his face.

"You men think you're gonna melt if you take a bath," she said.

He nodded his head in agreement.

Billie Jo dropped the towel on the table and shook her head.

The man got up from his table and walked over with his hat in his hand.

"James Butler Hickok, ma'am. Some call me Wild Bill. You're right about us, miss, we like whiskey but we have a reluctance to plain water."

"Heard of you. I'm Billie Jo Dobbs, and the two I sent to take a bath are Judge Fuller Newton and Digger. Where you headed?"

"Goin' back to Deadwood. Came out here to hunt buffalo with Bill Cody but there ain't none left. I see you and your friends are on horses, ya'll must be from around here."

"No, we're out from Kansas, goin' to see my Northern Cheyenne kin up in Montana. Just stopped off for a bath and some sleep."

"Lot of folks gettin' killed up there. You sure it's worth it?"

"Something I have to do."

"I understand that feeling." He stood up and, before he placed his hat back on his head, said, "Nice to meet you, Miss Dobbs," and walked back to his table.

A few minutes later, the front door swung open and two young dust-covered, long-haired cowboys walked in the room. One was tall and thin, wearing an Indian-made buckskin shirt, the other one short and scrubby-looking with a braided scalp hanging from his belt. They brushed themselves off and walked by a saloon girl folding bath towels waiting for two buckets of water on the stove to heat. The tall one grabbed her ass as he walked by. She knocked his hand away, wrapped two towels around her hands and picked up the buckets and carried them to the lean-to for the Judge and Digger.

"I need a drink," the tall one said and walked behind the bar.

"Me too," the shorter man said.

The one behind the bar picked up two glasses and poured himself and his friend a glass of whiskey.

The girl walked back in from the lean-to and went behind the bar and jerked the whiskey bottle out of the man's hand. He patted her ass again and laughed.

"How much for that," he said.

She pushed his hand away and ran out from behind the bar.

"One dollar," she said, standing on the other side of the bar.

"That for you or the whiskey," the tall one said, grinning at his friend.

"Whiskey," she said.

"We ain't payin' you nothin', ugly," the tall one said.

She ran out the front door and the stage manager, Walt, came back in with her. He was an old man with thin gray hair and a time-worn face.

"Put the money on the bar for the whiskey and leave," Walt said.

The short man drank his glass of whiskey and threw the glass against the wall behind the bar, knocking a pan off the wall.

"Ain't fit to drink. Ain't payin' you nothin'," he said.

"Then why did you drink it," Wild Bill said, standing up from his table.

"Who the hell asked you?"

"Pay the man and leave. No sense dyin' over a dollar."

"Awful big talk, mister, but this ain't none of your business," the short man said.

The tall one placed his hand on his pistol handle. "Damn sure ain't," he said.

Billie Jo stood up.

"Don't even," the tall one said. "Ain't none of your business, either, sweet ass."

The tall one drew, but Billie Jo drew first and cut him down before he cleared leather. Wild Bill did the same to the other man. The lean-to door flew open and Fuller ran in with Big Boy in his hands, a towel wrapped around him, aiming the shotgun at Wild Bill.

"No!" Billie Jo yelled. "Not him."

Wild Bill had both Colts pointed at the Judge, Digger behind him with his wet pants on and his Winchester pointed at Wild Bill.

"What happened?" Fuller said, still eyeing Wild Bill as he lowered the shotgun.

The stage manager and saloon girl poked their heads up from behind an overturned table and stood up.

"Them two was goin' to kill us," Walt said.

"Another pair of no-counts," Billie Jo said.

"And who are you," Fuller said, looking at Wild Bill, who still had the Colts pointed at the Judge.

"Bill Hickok."

"As in Wild Bill Hickok?" Fuller said.

"The one and only."

"Well I'll be damned, heard a lot about you," Fuller said. "Should'a known you don't start fights."

"Try not to, at least," Wild Bill said. "That young lady is the fastest gun I ever seen. Glad it wasn't me she was drawin' against."

"She is," Fuller said. "Growed up with a father just as fast that taught her."

"You know those two?" Billie Jo asked, looking at Walt.

"Nope, never seen 'em before," Walt said. "They rode in on Indian ponies. Probably ambushed some bucks for their horses and scalped 'em, goin' by what's on the little one's belt."

"Dig 'em a hole, Digger," Billie Jo said. "You're good at it."

Digger looked at them. "Okay, but everything they got is mine, including them horses."

"Sure," Fuller said.

"I'll go put the ponies in the barn," Walt said.

Digger grabbed them by their collars and drug both of them out the back door.

The Judge watched Digger drag the dead out and walked over to Bill.

"I've always wanted to have a poker game with you," Fuller said. "Read about your skills in the dime books."

"Alright with me but don't get mad when I win," Wild Bill said.

"You ain't got a chance, Judge," Billie Jo said.

"You actually a judge?" Wild Bill asked.

"For now, at least. So watch out, I might arrest you if you win," Fuller said and laughed.

Fuller grabbed a bottle of whiskey and two clean glasses off the bar and headed for Wild Bill's table, Billie Jo following. They sat down and Wild Bill pulled a deck of cards out of his shirt pocket and laid them on the table.

"You playin', Billie Jo?" Wild Bill said.

"No thanks, I'll just watch," she said and sat down.

"Alright if we play with my cards?" Wild Bill said.

Fuller stared at the cards. "You wouldn't cheat me would you?"

"Nah, they're not marked or nothin' like that."

"Okay, I'll trust you. You got a good reputation."

"Five or seven?" Wild Bill said, picking up the cards.

"Five-card stud," Fuller said.

"We got a limit?"

"Not unless you want one. Let's ante up twenty."

Wild Bill nodded and they both pitched a twenty-dollar gold piece on the table. He dealt the cards, picked up the whiskey bottle and poured himself a glass of whiskey. Fuller poured himself one of the same and picked up his cards.

"Gimme three," Fuller said.

"I'll take one," Wild Bill said.

Wild Bill dealt Fuller his three cards and then his one.

"I'll raise twenty," Wild Bill said and pitched another gold piece on the table.

Fuller frowned and tossed his cards on the table.

"I fold," Fuller said.

Billie Jo shook her head. "He's gonna clean you out, Judge."

Wild Bill laid his cards on the table face down and picked up the money.

"Guess that's enough for one night, Bill, if that's alright with you." Fuller said. "I better quit while I still have the shirt on my back."

"Okay with me," Wild Bill said. "Think I'll eat and get some sleep 'fore that long stage ride tomorrow. Good luck to you. All of you. Ya'll gonna need it."

Wild Bill went to pick up the cards when Fuller stopped him.

"Now that it's over, would you show me what you were holding," Fuller said. "Just so I can go out knowin' you beat me."

"Don't mind." Wild Bill turned the cards on the table face-up. "Two pair. Aces and eights."

"That's a good hand in any game," Fuller said. "I probably would've ended the night broke like Billie Jo said."

Wild Bill smiled, picked up the deck and put the cards in his shirt pocket.

"You sure would have," he said.

"At least I got to play a hand with you like I always wanted," Fuller said.

"Here," Wild Bill said, "keep the deck." He took the deck of cards out of his pocket and pitched them to Fuller.

Fuller snagged the deck and put them in his pocket. "Thanks. Gives me a great story to tell."

Wild Bill grinned then walked away. Before leaving the room he turned back and looked at Billie Jo. "Take care of yourself, ma'am," he said. "Wish we had more time."

"Me too," she said and smiled.

The next morning when Billie Jo and the others awoke, Wild Bill was already gone and dark clouds were rolling in across the sky.

Fuller came out of the outhouse cradling Big Boy in his arms, buckling his gun belt. Digger opened the cabin door and walked out chewing on a biscuit, Walt and his wife Bluebird behind him.

Two tough-looking men with sun-baked faces climbed up on the stage seat. The driver unwrapped the reins from the stage break and the other one sat down beside him on the stage seat and sat his double-barrel shotgun on his lap.

The stage driver snapped the reins and the horses broke into a gallop and they were gone.

Fuller took the cards out of his pocked and meticulously looked over the deck.

"Checking to see if they're crooked?" Billie Jo said.

"Somebody's gonna shoot his ass if they think they are," Fuller said as they all watched as the stage got smaller and smaller, disappearing on the trail. "We need to head for Custer's Rosebud encampment soon as we can. The Sioux and Cheyenne gettin' thick as flies 'round here."

"I don't want to ride with the army," Billie Jo said.

"Don't have much of a choice," Fuller said. "We stay here much longer we're gonna be dead."

"You right about that," Walt said. "Everybody comin' by here been tellin' us there's a big fight brewin' with the Lakota and Cheyenne. They movin' from everywhere to Sittin' Bull's camp on the Little Big Horn. One of the bravest chiefs, Crazy Horse, is leadin' 'em. The stage lines said 'close this place down and get.' We gonna skedaddle to the Rosebud as soon as I turn them horses loose. I'd like to ride with you if you don't mind?"

"More guns the better," Fuller said. "You're gonna have to travel light, though, we can't let you slow us down."

"The Indians see them ponies with that young fella they gonna pick him out and take a long time killin' him if they catch him."

Fuller gathered his cards and stuck them in his pocket, stood up and picked up Big Boy off the table.

"Everybody saddle up, we got to get. Turn them ponies loose, Digger. Walt's right."

"Them ponies you said I could keep?" Digger said. "Think you tricked me, Judge. Why didn't you tell me that before I dug the grave?"

"You wouldn't have dug the grave," Fuller said.

"Gonna remember that," Digger said.

# 15

They rode away from the station and soon after saw a dozen or more Sioux and Cheyenne riding in the same direction along a grassy ridge, out of range.

"Keep the horses walking. Don't run," Fuller said.

"Why don't they attack?" Digger said.

"Probably thinkin' we may be a decoy for soldiers to draw them in for an ambush. If they do head for us, that ravine to your left is where we'll fight them. We can't outrun them."

"That one on the white horse is waving a white flag," Walt said.

"That's their chief. Bet he wants to talk," Fuller said. "Think he would tell us to give them something like Bittersweet if we don't want to be scalped."

"You think we should?" Digger said.

"Over my dead body," Billie Jo said.

"That could happen," Fuller said. "Billie Jo, pull your Winchester and shoot the one on the white horse when I tell you to. We have to scare them."

"Ain't goin' to help me none with the Indians," Billie Jo said.

"You better if you want stay alive and keep your horse," Fuller said.

Bluebird rode up beside Walt and tugged on his sleeve, pointing to some blurred figures in the dust riding toward them.

Walt looked at where she was pointing. Dust curled up behind three riders heading straight at them.

"Yeah I see 'em," Walt said. "Don't look like Indians, though."

Walt spurred his horse and rode up to the Judge and pointed at the three riders.

Fuller nodded. "I see them. The Indians gonna see them, too."

The three riders were gaining ground rapidly. The Cheyenne on the white horse rode out from his band, raised his rifle and waved it.

"Now, Billie Jo," Fuller said.

Billie Jo cocked the Winchester, took aim and fired. The Cheyenne tumbled off the back of his horse. Two braves rode to him, picked him up and tied him across his pony. They took off at a fast gallop and the rest followed.

"They leavin' now," Digger said.

"If Indians don't have a leader they get skittish," Fuller said.

The three riders were close enough to recognize now through the dust.

"I'll be damned, it's Slate and his boys," Fuller said.

Slate rode up to the Judge and shook hands with him. Glover and Hatchet rode by and shook hands with Fuller then waved at Digger and Billie Jo.

"Whoever shot the chief made a hell of a shot," Glover said.

"Told Billie Jo to kill him," Fuller said. "We had to show courage."

"The Lakota and Cheyenne are comin' from everywhere now," Slate said. "Different tribes bandin' together, makin' Custer happy. He wants a big victory to give him a run at the White House next election. Think he may have bitten off more'n he can chew this time."

"You think so?" Fuller asked.

"Never seen this many in one place before."

"Looks like you scared them off, Slate. Good to see you," Billie Jo said.

"You scared them off with that shot," Slate said.

"Not many could make it from that far away," Glover said.

Hatchet nodded in agreement.

"Thanks, I guess," Billie Jo said.

Walt rode up with Bluebird beside Slate.

"Name's Walt Peterman, mister. You a scout?"

"Yeah, name's Slate. We're scouts for General Custer."

"Them Indians gonna be back with a lot more," Walt said.

"Yeah, you're right about that," Slate said. "They'll attack when you see 'em again. Hatchet, you and Glover pick up the point and find us a way out of here."

"You got it," Glover said and he and Hatchet rode away.

"How far we got to go 'til Custer's camp?" Fuller said.

"'Bout twenty miles, or so," Slate said. "But it may turn into a hundred if we have to keep dodgin' all them Indians."

"Custer know about them?"

"Maybe. He's got a lot of scouts out roaming the country, one of 'em was bound to have told him. We're gonna have to weave our way through the Indians to get back."

# 16

They worked their way back to the Rosebud without a fight and rode into the old fort. Several hundred soldiers were bivouacked in buildings left from a once-official army fort and the officers were in a scorched log building that had withstood an Indian raid five years prior. Cottonwood trees stood along the far bank of the Rosebud River for miles, helping to conceal the fort.

A sign at the center of the log building read:

GENERAL G.A. CUSTER - COMMANDING OFFICER

"That sign says he's a general. He's a colonel now," Slate said, "but everyone lets him keep the title. Was a war hero. Ya'll go down to the mess hall straight ahead for some grub and tell the mess sergeant you're with me. I'll let the General know you here."

"We'll do it," Fuller said.

"Heard a lot about Custer when I was growing up, Judge," Digger said as they rode toward the mess hall tent. Everybody said he was a hero."

"He should have been given a lot more credit for winning the battle at Gettysburg and the war. I was in his battalion during the war. Everybody's still trying to decide if him and his brothers are the bravest men they ever saw, crazy, or both. His brother won two Medals of Honor. Only five men ever done that."

"Well he better have a lot of brave ones with him now," Digger said.

"Him and his brother were the best cavalry officers in battle I ever saw," Fuller said.

"He know you?" Digger said.

"Yeah, he knows me. May not want to see me again, but he knows me."

"I don't think I'm going to like him," Billie Jo said. "He hates Indians."

"Only if they get in his way to Washington," Fuller said.

A captain with white hair rode in front of them, glanced at them with his cold blue eyes as he rode by. Billie Jo never took her eyes off him until he dismounted and entered the saloon at the end of the log building.

"That's Captain Frederick Benteen, Billie Jo," Fuller said. "Ain't him. Seen him now and then during the war. One of his friends told me his slave-owner papa said he hoped the first bullet fired by a rebel killed him dead if he was gonna fight for the Union. Benteen credits his preternaturally white hair to being in the seventh Cavalry with Custer, a man he loathes. He was a hundred miles away the day your mama was killed."

"You sure?" Billie Jo said.

"I am."

"There's the mess tent," Walt said, excited, and kicked his horse. He and Bluebird rode up to the tent and dropped off their horses. "I'm so hungry I could eat a bear playin' a fiddle," he said and hurried inside the tent.

Digger and Billie Jo looked at each other, confused, then looked at Judge Fuller, who just shrugged his shoulders.

"Well, let's go help him eat that bear, I guess," Fuller said. They all laughed and dismounted their horses and headed for their meals inside the mess tent.

When Slate went in General Custer's outer office, John Burkman, Custer's faithful striker, was sitting on a bench snapping a rag on Custer's shiny black cavalry boots. Custer's wolfhound dogs Tuck and Blench got up, staring at Slate.

"Lay down," Burkman said and they obeyed, Burkman keeping an eye on Slate.

"The general in?" Slate asked Burkman.

"Got a woman in there."

"Monahsetah?" Slate said.

"Yeah," Burkman said. "What you need him for?"

"Got some white folks with me. Need to tell him about them. See what he wants me to do with them. One of them was in his battalion durin' the war, a Captain Fuller Newton."

"He might shoot you if you bother him now," Burkman said.

"Yeah, she's the only Cheyenne he likes," Slate said.

Burkman nodded and grinned, and kept popping the rag on the boots.

Slate turned away and went back outside and walked down to the saloon. Inside, Glover and Hatchet were having a drink at the bar and Benteen was sitting at a table with two lieutenants. The saloon was off limits during the day to enlisted men.

Glover raised his glass toward Slate. "Want a drink?"

"Nah, not now," Slate said.

"You see the General?" Glover said.

"No, he's entertaining his favorite woman."

"Well we know it ain't Libby," Hatchet said. "Must be the other one."

"It is. He says she's a prisoner but I never seen a prisoner treated like he treats her," Slate said.

"Pretty obvious why," Glover said.

"The willing ones are kinda scarce out here, white or Indian," Hatchet said and downed the drink in his glass.

"What you care?" Glover said with a sly grin.

"Shut up, Glover," Hatchet said.

"Sorry," Glover said. "Had my head up my ass. Have a drink on me." He motioned and the bartended poured Hatchet another shot of whiskey.

"If the General gets a look at Billie Jo he'll run Monahsetah off," Slate said. "But I don't think it would do him any good. Billie Jo wouldn't give him the time of day, let alone herself."

"Heard a rumor he married Monahsetah in '68 and was already married to Libby before that," Glover said. "Some say he even had a kid by Monahsetah but there was another rumor that he was sterile from having gonorrhea."

"Captain Benteen started them rumors," Slate said. "Custer set up a fake marriage to satisfy her papa—Chief Little Rock—but he was killed the first day of the battle at Washita."

"Custer probably did it," Hatchet said and poured himself another shot of whiskey. "Crooked Leg was there, too, but escaped. I'm goin' to find that sonofabitch someday."

Fuller walked in the saloon and made his way to Slate and the boys.

"See the General, Slate?" Fuller asked.

"He's occupied at the moment," Slate said. "I'll go back later."

"Well, me and the men can camp out anywhere," Fuller said, "but I'd like to find a good safe place for Billie Jo and Bluebird. What's he doin' anyway?"

"Bangin' a Cheyenne woman," Hatchet said.

"Durin' the day?"

"Whenever he wants to," Glover said.

"Yeah, he makes the rules but they don't apply to him," Hatchet said.

"I'll try again. Ya'll wait for me here," Slate said.

"I'll go with you," Fuller said.

"Don't rattle him," Slate said, "he might run you off. Or worse."

Slate and Fuller walked out of the saloon together. When they walked in Custer's office, Burkman and the dogs were gone. Custer's shiny boots were sitting on the bench.

"Where's his sergeant," Fuller said.

"He wasn't here when I came in, just his striker. Only one he trusts," Slate said.

Fuller leaned forward beside Slate and knocked on the door three times.

The door came open and there stood Custer with just the top button buttoned on his pants, no shirt or boots on, with one hand behind him.

"Who the hell are you," Custer said, looking at Fuller. His once long blonde hair was gone. He had it cut short.

Custer had gained weight, his face showed some lines now. It had been more than a decade since Fuller last saw him. He remembered Custer as a twenty-three-year-old general in the war. Now, at thirty-six, his mustache had a touch of gray and drooped a little more and he had a slight belly pouch sticking out from his unbuttoned pants.

"Thought you might remember me," Fuller said.

"No, can't say I do," Custer said, sticking his head out the door. "Burkman!" he yelled. "Where's Burkman?"

"Wasn't here when we came in," Fuller said.

"You know Burkman?" Custer said.

"Yep, he was with you during the war," Fuller said. "And so was I."

"What's your name?"

"Captain Newton Fuller."

"Been a while. I do remember the name but your face slips my mind."

"Don't matter," Fuller said. "Slate brought us here. We need a place for two women and some protection from your horny soldiers, a lot like you."

"The last thing we need here is an insubordinate with a foul mouth," Custer said. "You and your boys are fired, Slate."

Custer started to close the door but Fuller stuck his foot in the way, blocking it from closing.

"General, we're not goin' anywhere," Fuller said.

Custer brought a Navy Colt out from behind his back, pointing it at Fuller. He had a quizzical look in his eyes like he wasn't sure what to think about this encounter.

"General, I brought him and four others in from the stage station at Hell Rock," Slate said. "The Cheyenne would have killed them. Two are women. What would you have done?"

"Same as you did," Custer said, shaking his head.

The door behind Custer came open and the beautiful Cheyenne woman Monahsetah, dressed in a traditional beaded rawhide dress, walked over to Custer.

"Go on to your quarters," Custer said and she walked past Slate and Fuller out the door.

"Come on in, have a seat." Custer dropped his hand with the Colt and laid the gun on his desk.

Slate and Fuller walked in and Custer sat down behind his field desk.

"Okay, what's the story? Why are you here? Looking for gold?" Custer said.

"No," Fuller said. "I have a young lady that's half Cheyenne. Her pa, a white marshal, was killed and she wanted to come back to join her Cheyenne family."

"Couldn't have picked a worse time," Custer said. "How old is she?"

"Twenty," Fuller said.

"She's full grown." He sounded surprised. "You dickin' her?"

Fuller jumped up and Custer grabbed the Colt and pointed it at him.

"Sit down," he said, pointing at the chair with the Colt. Fuller slowly sat back down. "She kin or something?"

"No. She's the daughter of a longtime friend of mine. He served in your unit at Gettysburg same time I did. Captain Lamont Dobbs."

"Don't ring a bell either," Custer said and pitched the Colt on the desk. "I have a tendency to fly off the handle sometimes, Captain, sorry about that. And Slate, you can forget what I said about firing you. As for the women, we can put them up in the family quarters with guards around the clock. You and the other men can find you a bed in a bunkhouse. We'll be moving out for a long ride when my scouts get back. We'll leave a garrison here to protect the dependents. You can hold up here if you have a mind to until we get them troublemakers on a reservation."

"I'll show them where things are, General," Slate said.

"Okay," Custer nodded. "Well, got to get dressed for officer's call. See you boys later."

Fuller and Slate stood up and Custer shook their hands.

"Sorry I didn't remember you, Captain Newton."

"That's alright, I remembered you."

Custer smiled. "We kicked the Rebs' ass, didn't we."

"We did, thanks to you," Fuller said.

When Fuller and Slate walked outside, the other four were waiting with their horses at the hitching post. Soldiers were stopping to get a good look at Billie Jo before they went on.

"Hope you got us a place to go," Billie Jo said. "I feel like I'm on display."

"You are. Slate will escort ya'll to the family quarters," Fuller said. "Don't go outside tonight, Billie Jo, it's more dangerous here than out there with the Indians. These are good soldiers but not necessarily good men. We'll come get you in the morning. I don't want you killin' anybody."

"Who was the Cheyenne woman that walked by here earlier?" Billie Jo said.

"Don't think she knows your bunch. Go on with Slate, I'll see you in the morning."

Captain Benteen walked out of the saloon with the two lieutenants. Billie Jo stopped and stared at him again.

"Not him, go," Fuller said, looking at Billie Jo.

"Good thing I trust you, Judge." She slowly turned away and followed Slate.

"Our turn, Digger," Fuller said. "If it's bunk beds I want the lower one. My back's been killing me for days from that long ride."

"Alright with me, I like the top bunk better," Digger said. "Way I slept back at the orphanage."

"Good, was hopin' you wouldn't give me no trouble."

"Did the General remember you?"

"No," Fuller said.

"You said he would."

"Well he didn't, Digger, now let's find a bed."

# 17

The bugler was sounding Reveille the next morning in the dark, except for lamp light coming from General Custer's headquarters, as soldiers raised Old Glory to the top of the flag pole.

General Custer was dressed in his white buckskin suit and wide-brim brown hat, holding the reins to his horse Dandy, saluting the flag as it went up; Burkman next to him, hanging on to the dogs' collars.

Troops were falling out for inspection. Judge Fuller and Digger came out strapping on their gun belts, watching the assembly of over six hundred men.

"Thought the top bunk was okay with you," Fuller said.

"It was," Digger said."

"Then why was you sittin' up in a chair asleep in the middle of the night when I went out to piss."

"Bed bugs. Never had that problem at the orphanage," Digger said. "Next time I'm gonna get my saddle and a blanket and sleep on the floor."

"You just have to move over and give 'em a little more room then go back to sleep," Fuller said.

"You got to be kidding."

Fuller pointed at the troops leading their saddled horses into position.

"Glad I'm not part of that. The damndest thing happened when Custer took over the seventh after his court martial. He colored the companies with same color horses. You see what I mean."

Digger watched the horses lining up.

"Black horses dressing down in a company, roans in another, bays in another and so on," Fuller said. "Most of the men thought he was goin' nuts."

"Maybe he is," Digger said.

"He's always been strange," Fuller said.

"So is Billie Jo. She thinks the Cheyenne can't wait to see her. She ain't gonna believe they don't until they run us off or kill us."

"Yeah, it's a lost cause on both counts," Fuller said. "Let's go check on Billie Jo. I'm sure all the hoopla woke her up."

They pushed their way through the soldiers and horses, watching where they stepped thanks to the hundreds of horses.

The night sentries had already been relieved at the family quarters. Billie Jo was standing just inside the doorway when they opened the door, her Colt on her hip.

"Was waitin' for you," she said. "Want to get away from this place quick as we can."

"What the hell are you all wound up about," Fuller said.

"Had a sergeant tell me they shot over six hundred Indian horses last week—some dead, some wounded—left them that way to keep the Cheyenne and Lakota on foot and make it easy to kill 'em. Most terrible thing I ever heard."

"The Indians do the same damn thing if they can't steal them." Fuller said. "You don't have a horse you can't move very fast. I've done some of it myself durin' the war. So you know, I got Bittersweet hobbled with a lock so you don't get any ideas 'bout leavin' 'til we figure how to get out alive."

"You lost your damn mind, Judge," Billie Jo said.

"I'm headed that way if you keep actin' like you're on a picnic."

"Am I a hostage?"

"In a way. Not gonna let you get yourself killed."

"The Judge ought to spank your ass like the kid you're actin' like," Digger said.

"Mr. Rose, you definitely ain't no rose," Billie Jo said. "This stinks."

"That's enough," Fuller said. "You both actin' like kids."

Slate walked up beside them. "Mornin', everybody," he said.

Billie Jo brushed past him and headed out of the building.

"Morning," Fuller said. "Feel like a bite?"

They walked out of the family quarters and made their way to the mess hall and picked up a mess kit. Billie Jo was already inside by herself a ways down on the other side of the long table with a cup of water.

"What's the matter with Billie Jo," Slate asked Fuller.

"Poutin' 'cause I won't let her go out there looking for the Cheyenne."

"Ignorance is bliss," Slate said.

Fuller nodded. "Custer found any Indians yet?"

"He's chompin' at the bit to kill 'em," Slate said. "Two scouts came back last night. They saw three or four tribes headed for the Little Big Horn River. Could be thousands of them."

"Custer believe them?" Fuller said.

"Don't know, he sent them back out with more scouts and said we was moving that way today so we would be ready when they found them again. He assigned me and the boys to Captain Benteen's battalion, saying Benteen needs more scouts, and divided up his command. He didn't give Major Reno a command, heard he don't trust him. In fact, looks like none of the officers trust Custer, either. Works both ways, I guess. He's convinced the Sioux and Cheyenne will run when they see us, determined to have a big victory to promote himself. Could get his ass kicked with Crazy Horse leadin' them, though."

"Could be, but with his luck, I doubt it," Fuller said.

"Got to go." Slate stuck a biscuit in his pocket and walked over to Billie Jo. "The Judge is right, Billie Jo. Stay here." Slate patted her on the shoulder.

"Come back to us," Billie Jo said.

"I will," Slate said and walked away.

"You goin' to eat any breakfast, Billie Jo?" Fuller said.

"Not hungry," she said.

"Suit yourself. Let's go check the horses," Fuller said and handed Billie Jo the key to the lock.

They crossed the street and made their way to the stables.

Digger walked up beside Billie Jo. "Sorry 'bout what I said."

"Forget it. I ain't no rose either." Billie Jo smiled at Digger.

"You're as pretty as one," Digger said.

"Well I declare, you do have a soft side, Mr. Rose."

Inside the stables, Billie Jo took the hobbles off Bittersweet and they fed and watered the horses. There was so much clatter from the soldiers yelling and the horses snorting it was like a twister had blown in. They had to hang on to their horses to keep them from running away.

Custer was mounted on his big horse Dandy and Burkman was behind him with Custer's dogs and his other mount Vic. Monahsetah was standing in the doorway of Custer's quarters wrapped in a multicolored Cheyenne blanket, her arms folded over it, watching Custer and his men.

Soldiers kept coming out of the family quarters kissing their wives goodbye at the door and grabbing their horses from the hitching post to join their company.

"What do think will happen to them?" Digger asked.

"Hard to tell," Fuller said. "Custer is a brave man but he's careless."

"What do you mean?" Digger asked.

"Well, best I can tell, he wants a big victory and is willing to take chances. So do the Indians. That's why there's been a lot of talk about them comin' from all over the country for a big battle. They want to chase the whites off their land. They don't know they can't. White prospectors discovered gold in the black hills and Custer made sure Washington knew it—to set up battles for himself. He wants to be president someday, like Slate said, and needs more glory. I doubt the flow of whites will end now, and the government won't stop chasin' Indians until they're all on reservations. A lot of both will die before that happens."

"Gonna wash some clothes," Billie Jo said and walked away.

"You need to give her more attention," Fuller said to Digger. "You're her age. Would help her get rid of them nightmares, too."

"Think I'd be better off holdin' a lit stick of dynamite."

Just then a woman and two kids came out of the family quarters and crossed the street to the commissary, then Billie Jo.

"You keepin' an eye on me, Judge?"

"Yep, thought you was goin' to wash clothes."

"Got 'em soakin'," she said.

"We'll get out of here 'fore too long," Fuller said.

"Maybe sooner than you think," she said.

"Why you say that?" Fuller asked. "What'd you hear?"

"The wife of Lieutenant Noels said her husband told her General Terry was moving his command to Custer and would come here after he meets Custer to escort everyone to the Yellowstone River to board the Far West boat and get them out of harm's way to Fort Lincoln by order of President Grant."

"Some of them wives may have some stories to tell Mrs. Custer," Fuller said.

"'Bout that Cheyenne woman?" Billie Jo said.

"Yep. Custer might have to stay with her when Libby runs him off."

"Want to have a drink, Judge?" Digger said.

"You better leave the whiskey alone and hold on to your senses" Billie Jo said.

"See what I mean, Judge," Digger said. "A lit stick of dynamite just waiting to blow things up."

"Come on, Digger, I'll get you some whiskey." Fuller smiled and patted him on the shoulder as they walked away.

# 18

General Custer rode up to Captain Benteen and Major Reno.

"We have to get close enough to attack before the Indians realize we're here," Custer said. "We're moving out."

Benteen and Reno formed columns and marched, leading over two hundred men each in different paths along the divide, with a pack train bringing up the rear. Custer declined two Gatling guns.

Sitting Bull climbed a hill overlooking Little Big Horn in a tearful appeal to the sacred Wakan Tanka to be victorious in the upcoming battle. He had previously had a vision of a large white cloud overcoming the dust storm of the approaching cavalry.

He never even knew who Custer was at the time.

Custer and his battalion ventured over the bluffs to get a look at the Little Big Horn while Benteen and Reno held up their troops to wait for Custer to begin engaging the Indians before they would move on. Later, the sound of gunfire could be heard coming from the other side of the river bluffs. Custer was attacking the enemy.

Slate, Glover and Hatchet rode alongside Benteen, who was moving at a very slow pace. Custer's adjutant showed up with a note from Custer that it was time for Benteen to move out.

"Don't you think we should pick it up some, Captain," Slate said. "We ain't goin' to be where Custer wants us. I know damn well you can hear what's goin' on."

"This is my command," Benteen said. "You and your jail-bird friends can ride out to him if you want. I have to think of my soldiers."

"That's what we're gonna do," Slate said. "You're either a coward or a hate monger. Either way, I don't have no use for you." The three of them rode off toward the sound of the rifles.

By the evening, the fighting was still going on as Reno and Benteen were trying to assemble the parts of several companies that had been left to retreat.

Lieutenant McDougall's pack train arrived at Reno's location and Reno greeted him drunk, with a whiskey bottle in his hand. Reno's troops were exhausted from fighting and running as he took them to tree lines along a ridge separating him from the bluffs where Custer was last seen with his battalion.

By late evening, it was getting dark and the battle had slowed down. One of the men watching from the opposite bank of the Little Big Horn was Billie Jo's Cheyenne brother, Two Moons. He had been part of the group that joined the charge with Crazy Horse, killing Custer and his brother earlier in the battle and finishing off the rest. All dead.

# 19

General Terry's column arrived during the withdrawal of the Indians that didn't stop to fight, and he didn't go after them. He sent out scout Little Face to find Custer and, when he returned, he reported to Terry that Custer and his battalion were all dead.

No one wanted to believe it.

General Terry sent Red Star to the Rosebud encampment to tell Lieutenant Noels what happened to Custer and to lead a detail to the Little Big Horn to help quickly bury Custer and his men.

Slate and his two friends found General Terry and told him of the reluctance of Benteen to rescue Custer and he said he would note it and dismissed them.

Slate and his boys topped a bluff and saw the Indians stripping and mutilating the dead. Nothing they could do now. They turned back to join General Terry's column for their own protection.

Red Star rode the rest of the day to reach the Rosebud. He found Lieutenant Noels and handed him a written order from General Terry. The lieutenant gathered ten officers to spread the word about Custer and to give assistance to the families of the dead.

Judge Fuller and Digger were in the saloon having a drink when First Sergeant Abbott came in and announced what happened to Custer and that no one could leave until Lieutenant Noels returned from a detail to lead them to the far west boat for transportation down the Yellowstone River to Fort Lincoln.

A few minutes after Abbott left, Billie Jo walked in the saloon.

"You hear?" Digger asked.

"Yeah, everyone's talking about it," she said. "I wonder if Slate and the boys were with Custer."

"They were assigned to Benteen," Fuller said. "Heard he's still alive, maybe they are too."

"That Cheyenne woman stole a soldier's horse and high-tailed it out of here," Billie Jo said. "Don't blame her, if she had stayed somebody would have cut her throat."

"Big victory for Sitting Bull," Fuller said. "But I think he just sealed his fate. Washington is goin' to come after him and his tribe with everything they got."

"What do you think we should do now, Judge?" Billie Jo said.

"It's time to leave this county for good," Fuller said. "You can't speak the language. The Cheyenne will disown you. We should have never come."

"They will see I'm Cheyenne."

"The Cheyenne's not the real reason you wanted to come anyway. You're still having nightmares and you wanted revenge. That's the real reason. You didn't learn to shoot for fun you learned with a purpose in mind. Your pa told me what was goin' on. He hated the Cheyenne for forcing him to leave and for not finding his son or the soldier that killed his wife. He knew he wouldn't live to go back but you could and would. That's why he made you so damn good with a gun. The boy's probably dead and so is the bastard that killed your mother. Give it up."

Billie Jo tried to hide a tear by covering her face with her sleeve.

"I wish you had never come. You didn't come to help me. You came to control me. I would have been better off without you." She ran out of the saloon.

"Well that put me in my place, I guess," Fuller said and poured another drink.

"I can't talk for you or Billie Jo," Digger said, "but I can tell you I think we should put all this to rest and figure out what we're goin' to do to get the hell out of here alive and talk about later later. I understand both your feelings. She has a place for you in her heart, but it's not the one you want."

"Don't think I have anything she wants," Fuller said.

Lieutenant Noels rode up to the Judge and Digger.

"I need you two to go with me to bury Custer and his men. His command don't want to do it."

"Were not in your army," Fuller said.

"Hell, I'll go," Digger said. "I'm a grave digger, anyway, Lieutenant."

"Didn't catch your name," Lieutenant Noels said, eyeing Digger.

"Name's Eli Rose. They call me Digger."

"Sounds like you're who we need, Mr. Rose. Pick up supplies for three days at the supply wagon and be ready to go in the next thirty minutes. We got a long ride. General Terry's orders said not to engage the enemy if we don't have to, so no freelancing."

"I'll be ready," Digger said.

The lieutenant nodded and rode off.

"He can't make you do this, Digger," Fuller said.

"Don't mind. Plus, looks like they need the help."

"You get back here as soon as you can."

"I will." Digger walked out of the saloon to the picket line to get his horse. He saw Billie Jo saddling Bittersweet. He saddled his horse and led him over to Billie Jo.

"Unsaddle that horse," Digger said.

"Why's that?" Billie Jo said.

"I'm goin' with Lieutenant Noels to bury Custer and his men. But I don't know whose goin' to bury you if you ride out of here alone."

"I can take care of myself."

"The Judge is back there waiting on you."

"Me and the Judge are through," she said.

"You know neither one of you mean that. You love each other, just for different reasons. There's not a man alive that wouldn't want you."

"Well, what about you?"

"Want to box me in don't you," he said and smiled.

"Yep," she said and smiled back.

"Me too."

"I'll be waitin'," she said.

# 20

After a long dusty ride, Digger and the detail followed the smell of death. They found the Custer battalion on a hill overlooking the Little Big Horn River. All of them naked, dead and horribly mutilated, Coyotes dragging off the bodies. Their skin glistening in the sun was like a winter kill of skinned buffalo. The smell of death covered the hill like a blanket. Some were found under others, presumably trying to hide under the dead before they were also killed.

They chased the coyotes away and found General Custer and his brother Tom halfway up the hill, side by side.

Custer had arrows shoved up his penis and ears, some of his fingers and toes were cut off. His stomach had been opened and intestines pulled out. His brother Tom was cut up from top to bottom like sliced bread shot with bullet holes. A pile of pistol shell casings were on the ground on Tom's right side. All of Tom's fingers on his right hand were cut off, most likely to take the revolver he was holding with a death grip when he died.

Even Digger wasn't prepared for what he saw and threw up when they found the scene.

General Custer and his brother Tom were buried in the same grave with an Indian travois placed over them and rocks piled on top to protect them from the coyotes.

It was guesswork as to who were the other men.

The detail could see miles of dust on the other side of the Little Big Horn as Indians moved away from the river, herding thousands of ponies north. Teepees were still standing on the far banks. Two troopers from the detail kept walking in circles, ranting and raving bout the defeat.

They jumped on their horses and one of them yelled, "We're gonna go kill what's left down there!"

Lieutenant Noels yelled back at them to stop, but they kept riding to the river. Noels and the detail mounted up and gave chase but couldn't catch up before they rode in and shot two women and a young boy.

Two other women ran out of a teepee and Digger recognized one as Star Morning and began to shout as he rode between the troopers.

One of the troopers aimed his rifle at Digger.

"Get out of my way, you Injun lover."

Lieutenant Noels rode up behind the trooper and cold-cocked him with his pistol butt.

"You disobeyed my orders," Noels shouted as the trooper fell from his horse.

Star Morning and the other woman were on the trooper with knives by the time he hit the ground. Digger jumped off his horse, yelling her name.

"Star Mornin', no, no don't," he said.

She looked up just as she was about to stab the unconscious trooper and saw Digger running to her. Digger grabbed the knife out of her hand and kicked the other woman to the ground, knocking her knife out of her hand.

"It's over. No more," Digger said, looking at Star Morning.

"Never over," Star Morning said, scrambling for her knife.

Digger slapped her across the face. "Stop," he said.

"We warriors like Buffalo Calf Road Woman and Pretty Nose that killed Custer man. Cut him up with his saber. We kill more."

"If you don't stop these men will kill you," Digger said.

She rubbed her cheek and stared at Digger.

"I saved you 'cause Billie Jo would have," Digger said. "Behave and I won't let them soldiers hurt you."

"Broken Moon alive?" Star Morning said.

"Yes, and she's near here," Digger said. "She's looking for the white-haired soldier that killed her mother."

"Remember White Hair," she said. "He fight with Crazy Horse."

"Where is he now?"

"Don't know?" she said.

"What's your name?" Digger asked the other woman.

"Two Horse Woman," she said.

Lieutenant Noels pulled up his horse beside Digger and the women.

"What's goin' on here, Mr. Rose?"

"They knew Billie Jo when they were kids," Digger said. "Think they might have some information we could use, I'd like to take them back with us."

"Don't have time to watch prisoners," Noels said. "Might be better to just kill them now. This is war, Mr. Rose."

"I'll take responsibility for them," Digger said.

"Alright, but if one of them gets out of line I'll shoot them both," Noels said. "Have them ride on one pony and don't turn it loose."

Digger ran down a pony on his horse and put Star Morning and Two Horse Woman on it and lead them away from the Little Big Horn.

Lieutenant Noels found Red Star and handed him a note.

"Give this to General Terry so he knows they are all buried," Noels said. "We're coming back to the Rosebud as ordered."

Red Star nodded and rode away.

The greasy grass waved goodbye to the detail as they left the Little Big Horn for the Rosebud.

Slate and his men came over a bluff and rode up to Noels. "Okay if we ride with you, lieutenant?"

"Where you supposed to be," Noels asked.

"No one has told us," Slate said.

"Okay, as long as you don't cause any trouble," Noels said.

"We won't." Slate dropped back to Digger.

"You're alive," Digger said.

"Think so, at least," Slate said.

"I helped bury Custer and his men."

"We saw them," Slate said. "Got there too late, though."

"You capture you some women?" Glover said.

"No, takin' them to see Billie Jo. They know her Cheyenne kin."

"You got any whiskey?" Hatchet asked Digger.

"Nope," he said.

Hatchet kicked his horse to a gallop, going trooper to trooper and asking if they had any whiskey, each one turning him away.

In the distance, they could still see a red sky from the dust of thousands of horses.

# 21

Late in the afternoon the Rosebud encampment came into view as the sun waited for its last breath of light to go out. The gates swung open as Digger, Slate and the others rode through. Women and kids were lined up to meet their men as they arrived.

Judge Fuller was standing on the walk outside the saloon, Big Boy slung on his back, grinning at Digger as he rode up leading the pony.

"Good to see you, boy. 'Bout time you got back," Fuller said. "See Slate and the boys made it, too. It's a good day."

"Not for Custer. Worse thing I ever saw," Digger said.

"I heard," Fuller said. "What you doing with them Cheyenne?"

"Run into them by accident at the Little Big Horn," Digger said. "Remembered Star Mornin', the other one said she was at Sand Creek with Billie Jo."

"How do you know that's true?" Fuller said.

"She told the same story Billie Jo did and remembers her and her brother."

"We'll let Billie Jo decide," Fuller said. "Think I just about convinced her to leave here for good, if you're going with us, but finding them two women may change her mind. Might just be better to turn them loose 'fore she knows and let them go back to the Cheyenne."

"Don't think I could do that, Judge, would always haunt me," Digger said.

"Yeah, I guess so," Fuller said.

Two detail troopers walked up and each grabbed one of the Cheyenne women with a tight grip around their neck and began fondling their breasts. One of the men had a thick beard and an even thicker country accent; the other one with the same accent, a thick mustache and long side burns.

"We'll take them squaws now, boy, you had your turn," the bearded one said, hanging on to Two Horse Woman, squeezing her breasts. "We gon' cut 'em up like turkeys after we finish for what they did to Custer."

Fuller swung Big Boy off his back and smashed the bearded one across the face with the butt of the shotgun. The man let go of Two Horse Woman and staggered back a ways, his smashed nose bleeding like the gunslinger did in the saloon. He fell to his knees, his eyes blinking and his head rocking back and forth like it was going to fall off.

Fuller jabbed the other one in the stomach as hard as he could with the barrel of the shotgun, he bent over gasping for breath and Digger pistol-whipped both of them to the ground.

A dozen or so troopers ran to Digger and started pummeling him with their fists. Fuller was swinging his shotgun, hitting anyone he could reach. Billie Jo showed up and fired her Colt twice into the air to get everyone's attention.

"Back off and leave them alone," she said, lowering the Colt to point it at the troopers. "Back off or I'll start killin' you."

A scrawny private put his hand on a knife on his belt. "You shoot anyone I'll cut your throat," he said.

"You won't last that long," Billie Jo said, "bringing a knife to a gunfight."

Digger wiped the blood off his face with his shirt sleeve. "Them two troopers was gonna rape and kill the women."

Billie Jo looked over and, after a moment, recognized a familiar face.

"Star Morning," Billie Jo said. "What are you doing here?"

"Come with Digger," Star Morning said.

Lieutenant Noels busted through the troopers and saw Billie Jo holding a gun on his men.

"Lieutenant," a private said, "Digger tried to kill Griswold and Hutch over them sorry Cheyenne."

"You attack my men, Mr. Rose?" Noels said.

"Was the other way around," Fuller said. "Your troopers attacked the Cheyenne women. They was goin' to rape and kill 'em."

Noels looked down at the troopers on the ground, blood all over them.

"Get them to a doctor," Noels said. Four troopers picked the men up and they staggered away holding on to them. "Sergeant Abbott, place Mr. Rose and Captain Newton here under arrest, and put the Cheyenne women in a private cell." He turned to Billie Jo. "And you, lady, put that damn gun away or I'll arrest you, too. Don't you know what they did to Custer?"

"Not them," she said, still holding the Colt on the troopers.

"Put it away, Billie Jo," Fuller said.

After a few moments she nodded and holstered the Colt.

"Gentleman, I'll take your guns now," Noels said and Fuller and Digger gave them to him. "All you men move out now, it's over."

The troopers moved away two or three at a time until they were all gone.

"Let's go," Abbott said, waving his revolver toward the guard house.

"What are we charged with?" Fuller said.

"Gonna charge your friend Digger for attempted murder, and you for assault and battery," Noels said. "Take 'em to the guard house, Sergeant Abbott. I'll file formal charges against them later."

"Sounds like we goin' to have a hangin'," Abbott said once they were out of ear-shot from the lieutenant. "You two should'a just let them men have some fun." He began eyeing Billie Jo. "Should put you in the brig, too, Miss Tight Britches. Might even do to ya what them men didn't get to finish with them Cheyenne."

"You bastard," Billie Jo said.

He grinned and stuck his revolver in Digger's ribs. "Get on over to the guard house," he said.

Several of the troopers that were in the crowd followed Abbott to the guardhouse.

One of them yelled out, "You where you belong, bunch'a no-goods sidin' with the enemy!" Another private in the crowd yelled, "Should put that bitch in the brig with the others!"

"I got other plans for her a little later," Abbott said. He locked Digger and Fuller in a cell and shoved the women into another one and locked it. "I'll pay you two a visit after we hang the others." He laughed and left the guard house, pitching the keys to the guard.

Billie Jo was standing at the bar window, looking in at Digger and Fuller.

"Why did you bring the women here, Digger? You knew what would happen," Billie Jo said.

"For you. Two Horse Woman was at Sand Creek when you were there, remembered you and your brother Two Moons. He's still alive, she says."

"I knew he was, he had to be," she said, looking relieved. "I think I remember her, too. Gonna find Slate." She hurried away.

"I know what she's thinking," Fuller said. "Woe is me."

An hour later, a voice was calling in the dark. "Hey in there."

In the next instant, four faces were pressed against the bars inside.

"So dark I can't see you," Digger said.

Slate stepped up to the bars and Billie Jo moved up beside him.

"I put the guard to sleep for the keys, gonna get you out of there," Slate said. "Overheard Noels saying he had to hang you or his men would hang him."

Slate stepped up to the guard house door, unlocked it, and then unlocked the two cells.

"Glover's holding your horses out back, your guns are on the horses," he said. "Swiped Big Boy, too, Judge."

"You bring horses for the women?" Digger said.

"Yeah, stole two strong ones," Slate said.

"Holy shit, we got to get," Fuller said.

"Hatchet is waiting at the gate to let us out," Slate said.

Hatchet spotted them riding hard toward the gate. He moved out of the dark and pushed the big timber through the gates to the ground, opening the gates just as they rode out at a hard gallop, the two Cheyenne women following closely behind on horses of their own.

# 22

They made a run through the woods by the light of the full moon. After several miles of running, they brought their horses to a single-file walk.

Slate pulled his horse up in some pine trees and waited for everyone to catch up.

"Don't think Noels is comin' after us. He's afraid he'll run into the Indians."

"Me too," Judge Fuller said.

"Yeah," Slate said. "Might as well wait for the sun so the Indians can see the Cheyenne women when we ride into the open out there."

They all got off their horses, took their rifles out of the saddle scabbards and sat down a few feet apart, hanging on to the horses.

When the sun came up they could see thick clouds of dust miles away, the Indians heading north instead of going east to the Black Hills.

"Wonder why they're heading north," Fuller said.

"To grandmother," Two Horse Woman said.

"What does that mean?" Digger said.

"Canada?" Slate said. "The Queen of England?"

"All I know is I got to find Crooked Leg before they get too far away," Hatchet said. "May have to go after him by myself."

"Damn, all you think about anymore is Crooked Leg and whiskey," Glover said. "You know you wasn't much of a Romeo anyway before he got ya'."

"If you don't shut your big mouth I may have to fix you, too," Hatchet said.

"Yeah, well, come and try," Glover said.

"Both of you, shut up," Slate said.

"He better back off," Glover said. "It wasn't me that scalped him and cut his balls off."

Hatchet jumped up and jerked his tomahawk out of his belt. Slate grabbed it and slung him down. "No," Slate said.

"I'm goin' to kill him," Hatchet said.

Fuller trained Big Boy on Hatchet. "I don't want to kill you," he said.

"He's sorry, ain't that right, Glover," Slate said. Glover didn't answer. "Tell him you're sorry, Glover, now, or I'm goin' to help him."

"I'm sorry," Glover said. "Don't know what got in to me."

"I don't think he's sorry but I'll take it for now," Hatchet said. "You want to take that shotgun off me, Judge?"

"You're not going to take it personal, are you?" Fuller said.

"No, got nothin' against you," Hatchet said.

Fuller dropped the barrel of the shotgun and Hatchet lead his horse away and sat down by himself. Billie Jo started walking toward Hatchet.

"Better to let him be, Billie Jo," Slate said.

She stopped, looked at Slate, and turned away and sat down by herself.

Hatchet raised his head and looked at Billie Jo. "You a nice lady," he said.

Billie Jo nodded and said a silent thank you to him that he picked up.

Digger went to Billie Jo. "How 'bout some company?" he said and plopped down beside her before she could answer and leaned his Winchester against a rock. "You goin' to stay with the Indians if you can?"

"I think, after I see my brother again and kill the man that murdered my mother, I'll go someplace where I can teach without fear."

"That's all goin' to take a long time," Digger said. "I guess you'll be an old maid by then."

"What do you care," she said.

"Well, you asked if I wanted you, and I said yes."

"I was just funning you," she said. "I didn't say I wanted you."

"No, you didn't. Thought we could get better acquainted, though, see if it might work. Was thinking the wrong thing I guess."

"Ain't time for no courtin' right now," Billie Jo said. "Bad time to be talkin' about it, anyway, with Hatchet here."

"If you say so," Digger said. "Thought I might ask you to get more personal and call me Eli, but that don't matter now."

Digger stood up and began to walk away when two bullets ricocheted off a rock and barely missed his leg.

"Take cover!" Fuller yelled and everyone dropped to the ground.

One of the Cheyenne women's horses bolted and ran out into the open and a rifle bullet put him down.

"Where did those shots come from?" Glover said.

"Couldn't tell," Fuller said.

"Two Horse Woman raised up a little and cupped her hands around her mouth, saying, "He'e uh hetaneo'o kase'e'e'he nave's e'e' Na'tse'heestaha."

"What the hell is she sayin', Slate?" Fuller said.

Slate concentrated, listening to her words.

"That she's Two Horse Woman...a Cheyenne...the wife of Little Hawk." Slate turned to Fuller. "Little Hawk is Crazy Horse's brother. He was with Crazy Horse at Little Big Horn."

"Everyone better save a bullet for themself," Digger said.

An Indian yelled at Two Horse Woman. She stood up and walked toward the voice.

A young warrior stepped out from behind a rock. He was tall, broad-shouldered with war paint on his face, holding a rifle.

"No shoot," Two Horse Woman said as she walked toward him. She stopped beside him and said something in Cheyenne. He handed her a skin water bag and she drank from it, continuing to converse with him in Cheyenne.

"What she say, Slate?" Digger said.

"Sounds like she's telling him about Billie Jo, wants them to lead us to Crazy Horse's camp."

"Probably to torture us to death," Digger said.

"She was a friend back then," Billie Jo said. "I think she's still a friend."

Star Morning stood up and walked over to Two Horse Woman and the warrior. Two more warriors dressed and painted like the first one appeared carrying rifles.

Billie Jo got to her feet and lead Bittersweet to them. They gave her a water bag and she drank and cupped some water in her hands for Bittersweet. She turned and waved to the others and everyone slowly lead their horses over to them. The warriors gave them water and they shared it with their horses.

The first warrior was walking around Bittersweet, talking to other warriors.

"He called Big Bear," Two Horse Woman said. "Wants your pony as gift. Take us to Crazy Horse camp."

"No, I can't do that," Billie Jo said.

"Do not anger them," Two Horse Woman said. "They give you another horse."

"No. She was a gift from my father."

Big Bear jerked the reins out of Billie Jo's hand.

"No one but me can ride her," Billie Jo said.

Two Horse Woman relayed what she said to Big Bear. He laughed and jumped on Bittersweet—she spun around, jumped, kicked and twisted, until she threw him off. He picked up his rifle and aimed it at Bittersweet.

Fuller drew down on him with the shotgun, both barrels cocked. "Tell him no, Slate," he said. "I'll kill him if he shoots that horse."

The warrior turned his head from Bittersweet to Fuller, staring at the shotgun. Everyone stood motionless. They standoff only lasted for about thirty seconds, but for everyone involved felt like hours. The warrior dropped his arm with the rifle and motioned to the other warriors to leave. They all disappeared into the trees.

"Bad thing to do," Two Horse Woman said to Billie Jo.

"You two are out of your damn mind," Slate said, looking back and forth at Billie Jo and Fuller. "You want us to die over a horse?"

"He couldn't ride her," Billie Jo said.

"Who cares," Slate said. "We got to get out of here now."

"Star Mornin' can double up with me," Digger said.

"Big Bear say not far now to Crazy Horse camp," Two Horse Woman said. "I go bring brother and Little Hawk here."

"I go too," Star Morning said.

"Why," Glover said to Hatchet. "So he can have the pleasure of killin' and mutilatin' us?"

Hatchet wasn't listening. He turned up his whiskey bottle and fell down trying for the last drop.

# 23

Once their horses were saddled, the two Cheyenne women gathered around Billie Jo.

"Wait for return, Broken Moon," Two Horse Woman said.

Billie Jo embraced her and then Two Horse Woman and Star Morning climbed on their horses and rode away.

Once they were gone, Glover turned to the others and said, "Why don't we run get the hell out of here, that squaw ain't gonna help us."

"She will," Billie Jo said.

"Bullshit," Glover said.

"Indian women don't have any say so, Billie Jo, they're property," Slate said. "Warriors trade them like horses. They have to do as they're told. That horse could have been our ticket out."

"Leave me alone," Billie Jo said. She pulled Bittersweet around, climbed up in the saddle and took off.

"Come back, dammit!" Fuller yelled. He ran to his appaloosa, jumped in the stirrup and took off after her.

"Wait for me," Digger said and followed on his own horse.

Hatchet started to climb on his horse but was stopped by Slate.

"No," Slate said, "we're stayin' here."

"We should go after them, Slate," Hatchet said.

"I hate to admit it, but he's right," Glover said.

"Looks like I'm outnumbered," Slate said.

"We can't go back to the fort," Glover said.

"I don't want to anyway," Hatchet said.

"What the hell, hit the saddle," Slate said.

They rode out of the tree line and lit out to catch up to Fuller and Digger. They could see their dust drifting across a yellow morning sky.

Fuller and Digger topped a small hill and spotted Billie Jo riding into a valley with teepees along a river bank. They heard the sound of horses behind them and saw Slate and his boys catching up and waited.

Slate and the boys rode up to them.

"Ya'll tired of living or something?" Fuller said.

"We got no place else to go," Slate said.

"I see her. She sees us, she stopped," Hatchet said.

They rode down the hill and galloped up to Billie Jo.

"You didn't have to come," she said.

"You didn't have to leave," Fuller said. "We may all be dead and don't know it yet."

"Here comes the devil's henchman," Slate said.

Four warriors were riding hell-bent for leather up the slope toward them.

"Should we kill 'em and run," Hatchet said.

"No, there's others that would catch us," Fuller said. "Hold your ground. Slate, when they get within hearing range, start telling them we're friends of Two Horse Woman, Little Hawk's wife. Everybody hold your hands up with no weapons. Billie Jo, take your hat off."

"Now's the time to save a bullet for yourself," Digger said.

As the warriors got closer, you could hear their horses puffing. They raised their rifles with the reins in their hands and kept coming.

"If they fire on us, shoot 'em," Fuller said. "We don't have a choice."

The warriors rode up. They had war paint on their faces, painted horses and a single feather in their head bands. One of them was Big Bear. They encircled the others, eyeing Billie Jo. They stopped and motioned for everyone to dismount.

"Well they didn't kill us yet," Fuller said. "Everyone get off your horse."

After they dismounted, two young warriors jumped off their ponies, took all their weapons, tied their hands behind their backs and gathered the horses. Big Bear grabbed the reins of Bittersweet and led her away on his horse.

"He's stealing my horse," Billie Jo said and ran to Bittersweet, her hands tied behind her back. Bittersweet reared up and jerked loose from Big Bear and trotted off a ways before stopping and looking back at Billie Jo.

Billie Jo whistled and called for Bittersweet and she ran to Billie Jo. Big Bear grabbed the reins away from Billie Jo again and placed a rope around Bittersweet's neck and whipped her with the reins.

"No, please," Billie Jo said and began to cry.

One of the warriors dressed in yellow buckskin grabbed Billie Jo, put a rope around her neck and led her away. Big Bear wrapped the reins tight around his hand, climbed on his pony and Bittersweet followed. The young warriors strung a rope around the necks of the others, mounted and led them down the dell to the river and teepees.

"That bullet won't do us any good now," Digger said.

One of the young warriors rode up to Digger, kicked him and shook his head no. As they entered the camp they saw an Indian with a feather bonnet step out of a teepee and look at them. A crowd started gathering around them.

"That's Crazy Horse over there," Slate said. "A warrior put that bullet scar on his cheek. Crazy Horse stole his wife."

"Got mine for the same reason, but with a knife," Glover said.

Big Bear slammed the butt of his rifle into Glover's gut. He fell to the ground, holding his belly. Before he could get up Crazy Horse walked up to him, helped him up, and gazed around at the others. He moved over beside Billie Jo, removed the rope from her neck and ran his fingers through her hair and smiled. He turned to the warrior that followed him, spoke to him in Lakota, and all the Indians laughed.

"What did he say," Digger asked, looking at Slate.

"He said it was a shame he already had too many wives."

Big Bear lead Bittersweet to Crazy Horse, gave him the reins and backed away.

"Who's pony this," Crazy Horse said in English.

"Mine," Billie Jo said.

Crazy Horse nodded. "You keep pony, woman." He motioned for a warrior to cut the ropes from her hands. He did and Crazy Horse handed her the reins.

"Well I'll be damned," Fuller said. "That ain't going to make Big Bear happy."

"Friends save Little Hawk wife and Star Morning," Crazy Horse said to the crowd and made a cutting motion with his hands. The warriors pulled the rope from around their necks and cut the straps from their hands.

Crazy Horse looked Slate over and spoke to him in Lakota. Slate spoke back in Lakota.

They were looking at Slate.

"He wanted to know if I was Indian. I told him yes," Slate said.

Two Horse Woman and Star Morning appeared from a teepee and walked up to Crazy Horse.

"We tell Chief you friends," Two Horse Woman said. "Want Broken Moon stay with us. Two Moon here soon."

"All can stay," Star Morning said.

The warriors with the rest of the horses rode up to them, leading their horses and carrying their weapons.

Fuller took the reins of his appaloosa and lead him over to Crazy Horse, handing him the reins, made a fist and patted his heart.

"Slate, please tell the chief he's the bravest of all warriors and should have a big strong pony," Fuller said. Slate translated the Judge's words to Crazy Horse.

Crazy Horse nodded and took the reins, made a fist and patted his heart.

"Enemy no more," he said. Fuller nodded and patted his heart again.

Big Bear drew his knife and charged at Fuller. Fuller sidestepped him and kicked him in the back and he tumbled over to the ground. He got up with his knife but Crazy Horse yelled at him and he dropped the knife and backed away. Crazy Horse yelled at him again and he went to his pony, mounted, and rode out of the village.

"Bad," Star Morning said. "He no come back to village."

"You disgraced him, Judge, givin' that horse to the chief," Slate said.

"He had it comin'," Fuller said.

"Don't forget, he'll come after you now," Slate said. "Watch your back."

"I will," Fuller said.

# 24

The yellow buckskin-dressed warrior pushed his way through the women and kids and stepped up beside Billie Jo.

"Who are you?" she asked.

"Yellow Nose. Kill many soldiers. Capture woman, belong to me." He grabbed Billie Jo around the waist and started dragging her away. Several warriors raised their rifles to the men in her group.

"Too bad she ain't got a gun," Glover said.

"Let me go," Billie Jo said, struggling to get free.

"Somebody got to fight for her or he keeps her," Hatchet said.

Digger stepped in front of the warrior. "She's mine," he said.

"Don't, Digger, he'll kill you," Billie Jo said, pulling on Yellow Nose's hands.

"You don't want to be his squaw, this is the only way," Digger said.

"You have to get Crazy Horse's permission to fight for her or they'll kill you," Slate said.

Digger looked at Crazy Horse. "Slate, tell him I want to fight Yellow Nose for her."

"He understood," Slate said.

Crazy Horse opened his hand and a warrior handed him a knife. They tied Digger and the Indian together at the wrist of their left hand with a rawhide strap.

"You don't know how to fight him, let me," Judge Fuller said.

"I know how to use a knife," Digger said.

The warriors formed a circle around them. Crazy Horse handed Digger the knife and Yellow Nose drew his knife out of his belt. Crazy Horse motioned for them to begin.

Yellow nose swung Digger around to his side, pushing him to the ground, and came down with his knife. Digger blocked his arm and rolled over on Yellow Nose's back and they fell side-by-side, each trying to stab the other. Digger grabbed Yellow Nose's arm with the knife, held on and spun him around and they fell to their knees, facing each other eye-to-eye. Yellow Nose swung his knife at Digger but barely connected. Digger grabbed Yellow Nose's knife hand with his left, came up from his hip with his knife, slashing Yellow Nose's throat, blood squirting out like a fountain. Yellow nose dropped his knife, his eyes rolling back in his head as he fell limp against Digger.

Digger cut the strap from their hands, pushed the body away and dropped the knife.

Crazy Horse took Billie Jo by the hand and placed it in Digger's hand. "Yours," Crazy Horse said. Three warriors picked up Yellow Nose and carried him away.

"We eat," Crazy Horse said and started back to his teepee.

"I don't know what to say…Eli," Billie Jo said.

"You just did," Digger said. "Nobody owns you."

"I know you want to be called Eli, so I will from now on," Billie Jo said. "Let's get you cleaned up."

"Ain't diggin' no more graves," Digger said.

"I know what you did, too, Judge," Billie Jo said. "No one will want my horse now."

"Have to play their game if we're gonna survive," Fuller said.

As they headed to the river, two warriors followed.

"They don't trust us," Digger said.

"I wouldn't trust us, either," Billie Jo said. "Thinkin' about ridin' Bittersweet outta here."

"Might as well follow for now," Fuller said. "Digger, you and Billie Jo water the horses and get cleaned up. Crazy Horse said it's time to eat, maybe we'll get something too."

"I ain't takin no bath," Hatchet said.

"We gonna get our guns back, Slate?" Glover said.

"Don't think so," Slate said.

Star Morning caught up to Digger and Billie Jo at the river bank with clean clothes for both.

Hatchet, Glover and Slate followed Billie Jo and Digger to the river. Fuller was taking his time to get there, it wasn't really a sight he wanted to see.

"You gonna give him a bath, Billie Jo," Glover said and smiled.

"Kind of," Billie Jo said and she as Digger wadded off into the river together.

"You can give me one next," Glover said, his grin turning into a broad smile.

Billie Jo looked at Glover. "I don't owe you like I do Eli," she said and smiled at Glover.

Glover nodded his head and laughed. He sat down on a rock next to Hatchet and said, "Maybe I'll just watch."

Billie Jo took Digger's bloody shirt off and washed his chest. He drew her to him and they stood there washing each other with their clothes on, Digger splashing water on her breasts. A crowd had gathered on the riverbank, watching them.

"You're goin' to have to come out of those clothes to get all that blood off, Eli," Billie Jo said.

"Well I ain't," he said. "I'll go down yonder to them cottonwoods to change when we get out."

Fuller sat down on the rock beside Glover. Eli and Billie Jo were caressing each other. He turned his head away, wiped a falling tear, and started dipping his hat in the water, washing his hair, face and beard.

Slate came to them leading Bittersweet and their horses and stopped beside Fuller.

"You goin' to have to find you a horse now," Slate said.

"I'll grab the first one I see when we ride outta here," Fuller said.

Two Horse Woman walked up. "Crazy Horse say come to teepee for food," she said.

"I could eat a skunk," Hatchet said. He jumped up and turned back toward the teepees, taking off at a fast pace, Glover following.

"I'll go tie the horses and meet you there," Slate said. Fuller nodded and they walked away in different directions.

Digger headed for the trees, Cheyenne warriors still following him, and Star Morning held up a blanket in front of Billie Jo and handed her clean clothes. Billie Jo stripped down put on the new clothes and left the dirty ones on the river bank.

Later, Star Morning packed a basket of food and blankets and asked Digger and Billie Jo to follow. She went to a nearby teepee, sat the basket down in front, and motioned for them to go in together. "You are one now," she said.

Billie Jo and Eli stood there looking at each other like it was the first time and walked inside.

"I'm not ready to be married, Eli," Billie Jo said. A tear was creeping out the corner of her eye and she wiped it away.

"Me neither," Digger said. "Don't know what's betwixt us for sure." He threw the flap back and walked out of the teepee and strolled away. Billie Jo came out. Fuller was watching and walked over to her.

"I don't want to hurt him," Billie Jo said.

"As Indians ya'll are already married," Fuller said. "Digger killed a man for you. That's good enough for them. It's good enough for me."

"I don't know what to do," Billie Jo said. "Not sure how he feels."

"I'll go talk to him," Fuller said.

He caught up with Digger and they both sat down under a tree.

"What'd she say?" Digger asked.

"Not much. She's kind of scared and confused," Fuller said. "We'll just have to keep taking care of her."

"You been doin' that all her life."

"Maybe it's your turn now."

"Don't know," Digger said. "Wouldn't want you mad at me."

"No, you're a brave young man," Fuller said. "That buck could have killed you."

"You're tough as a boot, too."

"Hate to say it, but if we had a fight, I'd lose."

"Unless you could get to Big Boy first," Digger said and patted Fuller on the shoulder.

"Yeah, getting old but not stupid," Fuller said and grinned. "Ya'll will make a decision and it'll be the right one."

"Hope so," Digger said. "What about you, Judge, you ever been married?"

"Yeah, back before the war." Fuller smiled, fighting back a tear. "A pretty little girl from a wagon train coming through town. Noticed her the first day they was there. She smiled at me when we saw each other on the street and I knew she was the one. They decided to stay and me and her got married later that year. Same kind of eyes and hair as Billie Jo, with lighter skin. May have had some Indian in her, I never knew. Was a happy time, for awhile." He paused, fidgeting with his hands, then continued. "She was killed two years later in a Sioux raid along with her folks. We never had any kids. Hurt too much to stay there. Sold the farm and moved on down to Kansas. Didn't meet Lamont until the war. Never found anyone else I wanted to marry. I think of her every time I look at Billie Jo. Might be why I cotton to her so much."

# 25

The next morning, Crazy Horse had shed his war bonnet and was dressed to fight, sitting on the appaloosa Fuller had given him, warriors gathering around him a hundred strong.

"What's he going to do, Slate," Judge Fuller said.

"Fight," Slate said. "He'll fight the troopers to the death right here. Him and Custer was in the same battle once before Little Big Horn but didn't come to blows with each other. History will remember them the most."

"I don't know 'bout you, but I'm goin' to get the hell outta here, guns or no guns," Hatchet said.

"Me too," Glover said.

"Go get Billie Jo, Digger, we better skedaddle while we got a chance," Fuller said. "Oh, and far as you and Billie Jo, if you walk away from a woman like her you don't deserve one."

To their surprise they saw Billie Jo come out of the teepee, plop down on the ground like her legs had given out, her knees folded with her arms around them and her head dropped in her arms. A most unusual sight, both Digger and Fuller were thinking.

"What's the matter with her," Digger said and ran to her, Fuller following. Slate and his men walked up behind them.

"What's wrong?" Digger asked Billie Jo.

She raised her head up wiped her tears. "Star Morning said Little Hawk and Two Moon were captured by the soldiers. They tied them to a tree and burned them alive. Why do they hate each other so much? When will it end?"

"You had to see it for yourself," Fuller said.

"That's why Crazy Horse is dressed to kill," Slate said. "He may start with us."

Crazy Horse rode up to Slate and Fuller. "Go to kill soldiers," he said. "I come back, you here, you die."

"We go now," Slate said.

"No guns," Crazy Horse said and rode away.

Two Horse Woman and Star Morning came out of the teepee.

"We hear," Star Morning said and hugged Billie Jo. She gave Billie Jo a rolled and tied blanket, holding a hand to her lips to be quiet. Billie Jo nodded.

"I will always remember you," Billie Jo said.

"Yes, go now," Two Horse Woman said.

They all headed for the horses. Fuller grabbed an Indian pony. They bridled and saddled the horses as quick as they could and mounted. Billie Jo tied the blanket behind Bittersweet's saddle and they took off.

They rode at a hard gallop until the horses began to wheeze, stopped on a bluff and looked back. In the distance they could see dust billowing into the sky miles away as Crazy Horse and his band rode toward the Rosebud where Noels and his troops were staying.

"I thought we were done for," Digger said.

"May still be," Fuller said. "The odds are against us with no water, food or guns."

"Did I tell you it was two women killed Custer with his own saber," Digger said.

"Where'd you hear that?" Fuller asked. "I heard it was Big Nose, a man."

"No, it was Pretty Nose, a woman, with another named Buffalo Calf Road Woman. Star Morning told me. They were warriors, rode with the men and everything. One of them still has his saber."

"Might better keep this between you and me," Fuller said.

Billie Jo rode up.

"Got something in this blanket," she said and untied the blanket on Bittersweet and dropped it to the ground. It unrolled and Big Boy was laying on it with six shotgun shells.

"Holy shit," Fuller said. He slid off the pony's back, picked up the gun and the shells and climbed back on the pony, holding Big Boy.

"Star Morning put it there," Billie Jo said.

"Knew she'd help us," Digger said.

"There's a crow village on the Yellowstone River that may be a place we can get food and guns," Slate said. "It's a two-day ride but we're sittin' ducks out here."

"Then that's where we'll go," Fuller said. "If you think they'll leave Billie Jo alone."

"They have Cheyenne living with them. Me and my mama lived with them," Slate said.

"I'm okay with it. Let's go," Billie Jo said.

"I don't care where we go," Hatchet said. "Let's just get out of here."

"Yeah," Glover said, "it's a miracle we're not already dead. Let's get."

# 26

They rode all night across a hot barren prairie with no food or water and the morning sun was quickly taking away what little strength they had left. The horses were dropping their heads and taking shorter steps. Bittersweet's ears perked and she started shaking her head, pawing at the ground.

"Bittersweet smells water," Billie Jo said.

"That's just wishful thinkin'," Digger said.

"Give her her head," Judge Fuller said.

Billie Jo loosened the reins around the saddle horn. Bittersweet began walking toward an unusually green mesquite bush on a small hill. Everyone dismounted and followed, leading their horses.

When Bittersweet got to the bush she began to paw at it, pulling it loose from the ground, and a tiny trickle of water oozed out of the roots. The other horses' ears perked up.

Digger dropped down off his horse to the ground, found a stick and dug under the bush. Mostly just dirt.

"Looks like it trickled down from them rocks," Hatchet said, looking up the hill.

They walked up to a rock formation and saw a small pool of water bubbling up from a ground bowl underneath the rocks.

"An artesian well," Slate said.

"If it's not alkali," Glover said, pointing at a skeleton lying against a rock not far from the water.

"I'll taste it," Digger said.

"No," Billie Jo said.

"Back off, young'n, I'll do it," Hatchet said, pushing Digger aside. He walked over to the skeleton. "Looks like there's a hole in the chest, might not've been the water killed 'em." He stuck a finger in the water. "It's cool." He put his face in the water, drank and raised up and shook the water off. "It's alright."

The others all dropped to their knees and began drinking, then let the horses drink, then got their canteens and goat bags and filled them, and finally wrung out their bandanas in the water and wiped their faces and tied the bandanas around their necks.

"No time for a bath this time, Billie Jo," Fuller said and grinned.

"I might anyway," Billie Jo said.

"Go ahead, we'll watch," Glover said.

"Don't think so," Digger said.

"You gettin' real personal with Miss Billie Jo now," Glover said.

"If I need to," Digger said.

"How far you think we are from the crows now, Slate?" Fuller said.

"Been makin' good time, maybe 'fore dark," Slate said.

"What's all the pictures and signs on them rocks say?"

"Some of them say Kill Soldiers, Water Spirits from the Gods, Forever Water, Finger Rock, mostly markers like that."

"Gonna remember where this well is if I ever need it again thanks to a horse we keep trying to get rid of," Fuller said. "We'll get a little rest before moving on again. Keep your saddles on, we may have to leave in a hurry."

"It might be now," Digger said, looking out across the barren country. Three Indians were riding straight for them about a mile away.

"They must know about the water," Billie Jo said.

"Hatchet, get the horses out of sight. Everyone else, find a hiding place," Fuller said. "Let them come in and I'll blow their heads off 'fore they know we're here."

"Looks like Sioux," Hatchet said as he lead the horse behind the rocks.

Fuller moved tight against the rocks. Digger stood behind him. Slate and Glover positioned themselves on the other side. Billie found a spot near Hatchet.

"Help me hang on to the horses, Miss Billie," Hatchet said.

"Me and Slate will be ready to take 'em down if you cover us, Judge," Glover said.

The sound of the horses got louder and louder until the first one rode in. The other two were close behind. Fuller stepped out from the rocks and fired. The first warrior went down dead with his horse. The other two turned their horses to run. Fuller shot their horses out from under them. One scrambled to his feet, running to his lost rifle. Slate beat him to it and put two shots in his head. The other one spotted Hatchet and Billie Jo and shot Hatchet in the chest. Glover tackled the warrior, jerked the rifle from him, and was about to shoot when he stopped.

"Crooked Leg," Glover said.

Fuller ran up and Glover grabbed Big Boy from Fuller and stuck the shotgun tight against Crooked Leg's crotch and pulled the triggers, blowing off the lower part of his body. Glover dropped Big Boy and ran over to Hatchet, now lying on the ground. Glover raised him up in his arms.

"That was Crooked Leg," Glover said. "I blew him apart, balls and all."

Hatchet showed a faint smile and squeezed Glover's hand, then closed his eyes and died.

With Hatchet still in his arms, Glover rocked him back and forth. "You skinny little bastard, you let that sonofabitch kill you."

Slate placed his hand on Glover's shoulder. "He died happy, Glover. You settled the score for him."

"He was a good man," Billie Jo said.

"We'll wrap him in a blanket and find a better place to bury him in the morning," Fuller said.

Slate walked up and handed Billie Jo a Winchester. "I gave the other one to Digger."

"I got just one shell left for Big Boy," Fuller said.

"One of them was Big Bear, Judge. Knew he'd come after you," Slate said to Fuller. "Crooked Leg must have heard about Hatchet being with us. No tellin' who the other one was, though. I'll go help Glover get Hatchet's body ready, help hurry this along."

"Better search the horses for food and weapons before we ride, too," Fuller said. "If there's any Indians around they definitely heard all that commotion."

# 27

Along the way, they stopped before daylight at a rock pile and waited for dawn to bury Hatchet. Digger dug out a small depression with his bare hands and they covered him with rocks. Billie Jo picked some flowers growing under a bush, wrapped them in a wet bandana, and laid them on his grave.

Slate walked over to Billie Jo. "Hatchet would have liked the flowers," he said.

"No one ever told me who did those horrible things to him."

"He was a soldier captured by the Sioux. They strung him up like a butchered buffalo, scalped one side of his head. Crooked Leg stripped him down and gathered a crowd of warriors to show what he did to soldiers and cut him…in a private place. He left him to die and went to join Sittin' Bull's tribe. For reasons

Hatchet never knew, an old squaw cut him down, sewed him up and nursed him back to health. He's been lookin' for Crooked Leg ever since. Stayed half-drunk all the time out of pain and anger. He was good with a gun. And a hatchet, as you might have guessed. Shame he didn't live to see what Glover did to Crooked Leg. His real name was Edman Smith, but no one except us here today will ever know now."

Billie Jo wiped a tear from her eye and sat silent. After a few minutes she asked Slate, "What about Glover?"

"That's the only name he's got. His wife and kids were murdered durin' the war. The three of us met in a saloon after the war and fought our way out after some slave dealers wanted to make Glover a slave again."

"Think the crow village will be a good place to go?"

"Think so," Slate said. "Go a long way back with them. Spent my early years there with my Cheyenne mama when my pa was soldiering, 'fore he got himself killed."

"Then you speak Crow, too."

"I know what they're sayin' for the most part," Slate said.

"She still there?" Billie Jo asked.

"No, died some years ago. Why I ain't been back for such a long time."

Judge Fuller walked up to Hatchet's grave and took off his hat and everyone joined him.

"May you rest in peace, Hatchet. You were one hell of a warrior," Fuller said and put on his hat.

They all mounted up and rode on.

It was late afternoon when they saw the Crow village along the Yellowstone River.

"Ride in with empty hands over your head," Slate said.

As they reached the edge of the village a woman ran into a teepee. A strong-looking young Crow warrior came out carrying a Winchester and tomahawk and stood in front of them as they rode up. The entire tribe began to gather around them.

"That's the chief's son," Slate said. "Stay on your horses until he tells us to get down." Slate gave him a sign meaning peace.

Warriors started shouting, "Absoroka, Absoroka."

"What're they sayin', Slate?" Digger said.

"They're telling the others that we're soldiers," Slate said. He turned back to the warriors and recognized one of them. "Running Deer?"

"Been many moons, Slate," Running Deer said.

"It has," Slate said. "Where's Standing Buffalo?"

"Chief die, tribe make son chief."

"Sorry to hear about your father, he was a good friend," Slate said. "We were hoping to come to camp with you, if we can?"

Running Deer pointed at Bittersweet. "Give pony, gift," he said and grabbed Bittersweet's reins and motioned for Billie Jo to get off. She did, reluctantly.

"Have something better," Fuller said. "Can I get down?"

Running Deer nodded his head yes and Fuller dropped down, lifting Big Boy's strap from the saddle horn. He cracked the breech to show Running Deer. He closed it and handed it to him with the last two shells he had.

"We keep the horse and give you this," Fuller said. "No more like it."

Running Deer turned the shotgun over and over then handed it back to Fuller and tightened the reins on Bittersweet.

"Look," Fuller said to the chief and pointed Big Boy at a big sapling. "Shoot, you see, big gun." Fuller handed it back to Running Deer. "Go on, shoot."

Running Deer put the shotgun to his shoulder, pointed it at the tree and pulled the trigger. The blast rocked him back and the tree splintered into pieces.

Running Deer looked at the tree and then the shotgun. "Good," he said. "Big gun. Bullets?" He held out his hand.

"Have to get you some more," Fuller said.

Running Deer dropped Big Boy on the ground and walked off with Bittersweet.

"Let him have her," Fuller said. "We've got no place else to go. I'll get her back."

"Looks like you lost her for sure this time," Digger said.

"Don't cause any trouble," Slate said. "He just told his wife to get us a teepee ready."

Fuller picked up Big Boy and brushed it off, looking over at Bittersweet.

"I'll get her back."

# 28

Miles away, on the Little Big Horn River, the crew of the Far West covered the eighty-foot vessel's lower deck with thick fresh green grass from bow to stern, stacked medical supplies around the deck loaded with fifty wounded men. A stall had been built for Comanche the horse, the only survivor of Custer's battalion.

They draped the boat in black and lowered the flag to half-mast. They stacked cord wood and grain along the sides of the boiler iron in front of the pilot house to protect the boat from the unpredictable currents and sandbars of the rivers. A tarpaulin was placed above the furnace to prevent the windows from becoming mirrors at night when vision was limited to glimpses of the river as the boat would speed down the Little Big Horn, Yellowstone and Missouri rivers to Bismarck and Fort Lincoln.

General Terry instructed Captain Marsh to wait three day before sailing to give him time to get the word out about Custer to the country.

After the three day wait, they sailed down the Little Big Horn River on a thirty-mile voyage to the Yellowstone River and continued in pouring-down rain until they docked at a crow encampment on the Yellowstone River around midnight. They blew the whistle, woke the village and they all ran to a familiar happening place to get food and tobacco from the Far West crew.

Billie Jo and the gang woke up, grabbed the Winchesters and ran outside, thinking they were in a fight. The beastly inebriation came to a stop and dropped the gang plank, shining a light on it as Captain Marsh—wearing his Far West cap, a bandana around his neck, and that stern look he always had—came ashore carrying a box of cigars for Chief Running Deer.

His crew unloaded twelve dead troopers for burial. He spotted a group of strangers coming toward him, placed the cigar box under his arm and waited. "What you doin' here," he said.

"It's a long story," Judge Fuller said. "Can we get a ride to wherever you're headed?"

"Don't have much room left," Marsh said. "Carrying thirty-seven wounded, a horse and crew. How many are there in your bunch?"

"Five."

"Are you wanted by the law?"

"No," Fuller said. "We had a little disagreement with a Lieutenant Noels over two Cheyenne women his troops were trying to rape and murder."

"Heard of him," Marsh said. "He was killed and four of his men wounded by Crazy Horse and his warriors when they was bringin' families to my boat."

"We can pay," Billie Jo said.

"If you knew Noels did you know Custer?" Marsh said.

"I was on burying detail with Lieutenant Noels," Digger said. "I buried Custer, and his brother Tom, along with a lot of others that day."

"You did?" Marsh said. "In that case, everybody get on board. This ride's free. We're leavin' at dawn."

"Captain, you got any eight-gauge shotgun shells?" Fuller said.

"You won't need a gun with us," Marsh said.

"Need to give them to the chief as a gift."

"Go on board and ask for First Mate Snyder, he'll let you know what we've got," Marsh said.

"Snyder," Fuller said, repeating the name.

"Yes, and tell him I said to make room for five more passengers. I have to take these cigars to Running Deer personally," Marsh said and walked away.

"Snyder? You don't think it could be any of Jeb's kin, do you?" Digger said.

"Nah, couldn't be," Fuller said. "I'm goin' to get those shells. Ya'll get ready."

"Why does it matter now?" Billie Jo said.

"After all the trouble we've had over Bittersweet I'll be damned if I'm goin' to leave her."

"They won't let you put that horse on the boat," Glover said.

"They already got one horse on there," Fuller said. "What would it hurt to have one more?"

Billie Jo leaned over and kissed Fuller on the cheek. "I'm just now realizing how much you mean to me," she said.

"Like a father?" Fuller said.

"Like a father," Billie Jo said and smiled.

"Good enough for me," he said and headed for the boat.

"Watch out for Snyder," Digger yelled.

Fuller shook his head up and down and kept walking.

Fuller was back within the hour with two boxes of twelve-gauge shells, fetched Big Boy and went looking for Chief Running Deer. He found him with Captain Marsh and waited for the captain to leave.

When March left, Fuller showed the chief the shells but he didn't offer to give Bittersweet back.

"Keep both," the chief said.

"No, that's not the deal," Fuller said. "You said you'd take the gun for the horse if I got shells."

Running Deer kept walking.

"I'll throw in two horses with the big gun and bullets for the pony," Fuller said.

Running Deer shook his head up and down. "I do," he said.

"Good. You smart, Chief," Fuller said.

Fuller walked up to Billie Jo, leading Bittersweet.

"What you doin', lettin' me say good bye?" Billie Jo said.

"Nope, I got her back like I said I would."

Slate and Glover saw Fuller with Bittersweet.

"See you got her back, now keeping her is the trick," Slate said. "Me and Glover decided we ain't going. That might free up some space, help you negotiate, but to tell the truth, I don't think you're goin' to get that horse on board. So if they won't let her go we'll take good care of her as long as we live, promise."

"I appreciate that, but why ya'll stayin'?" Billie Jo said.

"This is the only home I ever knew," Slate said. "Feels good to be back. And Glover likes it here, too."

"Never knew anyone I felt more comfortable with," Fuller said.

"Me too," Digger said.

Slate and Glover nodded their heads.

"Well, here goes," Fuller said, "got to find the captain."

"Let us know," Slate said.

Fuller left Bittersweet with Billie Jo and went on board looking for Captain Marsh. He found him in the pilot house on a cot with his boots off, a lamp lit on a side table.

"Sorry to bother you, Captain, got one more thing to talk to you about."

"You get the shells," Marsh said.

"Yes, thanks, there's something else."

"What?"

"I have a special horse I need to take with us. Since you have one on board I thought one more might be alright."

"No, I can't take anymore. Can't be as special as the one I got," Marsh said. "He's the only livin' thing from Last Stand Hill."

"No, she's not special in that way, but she was a gift from Billie Jo's dead pa, Marshal Lamont Dobbs. I promised him I would take care of her and the horse."

"Sorry to hear that but I can't take on another horse."

"I think you're doing a great thing, Captain, and that's what I'm trying to do. The horse I have is most likely one of a kind, with those markings she has. I doubt you'd ever see another one like her."

"I can't take another horse, that's that," Marsh said. "Go round up your people if you want to go with us."

"Captain, the horse means everything to that young woman. I helped raise her and love her dearly. This may be the last thing I can ever do for her. Please, I'll pay for it or whatever you want me to do."

"You're a persistent cuss," Marsh said. "I shouldn't do this but you bring her on board and stay with her in the stall 'til we get to Bismarck. That's where we're unloading Comanche. If anything happens to him before we get there I'll throw you and your horse overboard."

"Understood, thank you very much," Fuller said and left the captain on his cot.

# 29

Before the sun could climb over the high mountains, the Far West was sailing down the Yellowstone River to the Missouri on its way to Bismarck and Fort Lincoln.

Judge Fuller was sleeping on hay in the stalls with Comanche and Bittersweet separated by one long pole, Digger and Billie Jo asleep on cots in the pilot house and Captain Marsh directing the course of the Far West.

It was now early July, and the Far West had docked across the river from Bismarck to unload the wounded into the hospital.

Fuller lead Bittersweet down the gang plank with Digger carrying the saddles.

"Thanks for giving us a ride, Captain," Fuller said.

"You're welcome. Good luck to you." He walked back up the gang plank.

"Now what?" Digger said, looking at Fuller.

"Find some food and clothes, and horses for me and you," Fuller said.

"I still can't believe you got Bittersweet on the boat," Billie Jo said.

"I'll take the first Colt she has," Fuller said.

"He's yours," Billie Jo said.

"Here," Fuller said and handed Billie Jo the reins. "I even saddled her for you."

"You did everything right," Billie Jo said and smiled.

"Well, not quite. The twelve-gauge shells won't fire in the eight-gauge. I was running a bluff. Only hand I had to play."

Billie Jo and Digger looked at each other and laughed.

"Glad you didn't tell us," Billie Jo said.

"Slate knew but he backed off when he saw what I was doing."

"Hope the chief won't take it out on Slate and Glover," Billie Jo said.

"Slate knows how to handle himself," Fuller said, "Time to move on. I see a sign across the street at the Mariner Hotel that says hot baths, Billie Jo. And a saloon next door, Digger."

"I hear you," Digger said.

"Give me some money, I need some clothes," Billie Jo said, holding out her hand and handing Digger the Winchester. "Don't get too drunk."

"See what I mean, Judge," Digger said.

"Yeah, but it's worth it," Fuller said.

Billie Jo tied Bittersweet to a hitching post and headed for the mercantile store.

Fuller and Digger walked in the saloon. Digger dropped the saddles by the door and they went to a table where men were playing poker.

Two hours later, Billie Jo came out of the bath house dressed in a frilly red dress with white lace trim, her long shiny black hair flowing down to her waist. When she took a step you could see the white high-top-laced shoes she had on. She walked in the saloon to the table where Digger and Fuller were playing cards with three other players, all wearing Far West caps. Digger was staring at his cards and Fuller had his back to her.

Billie Jo placed a hand on Fuller's shoulder. "How much money you lost," she said.

"None so far," Fuller said without looking at her. "Won two hundred, my lucky day."

Digger looked up and dropped his cards as his hat fell off. He looked at Billie Jo and swallowed hard. "What in the world," he said.

The three other players laid their cards on the table, all eyes on Billie Jo except for Fuller, who was still looking at his cards with his back to her. He looked up and saw the others in a fixed stare over his shoulder. He turned around and saw Billie Jo, jumped out of his chair and walked around the table and stopped in front of her.

"You're the prettiest woman I ever seen," Digger said.

"Thought it was time to dress like a lady," Billie Jo said.

"Well you damn sure did," Fuller said.

"How much did you say you won," she said.

"Two hundred," Fuller said.

"You weren't playing with Bill's card were you?" she said and smiled. "You and Eli go buy you some clothes and take a bath."

"We have to?" Digger said.

"Yes, now," she said.

Fuller and Digger picked up their money and put it in their pockets. Digger picked up the Winchester leaning on the wall.

"See, I told you she would make us take a bath."

"You just can't say no to her," Fuller said.

"Nope," Digger said, looking at Billie Jo. "Sure can't."

# 30

Later that day, they were sitting in the dining room of the hotel dressed to the hilt. Billie Jo in her bright red dress, Digger and Judge Fuller with a fresh bath and haircut, both wearing white shirts with a black string tie and new black Stetsons hanging on a nearby hat rack.

"I want a big thick steak," Digger said.

"Me too," Fuller said. "I kind of like these gentleman's duds. May have to get some more."

"You do look like gentlemen," Billie Jo said. After a few moments her smiled dropped.

"I known now I can't stay with the Cheyenne, Judge," she said. "Should have listened to you."

"Experience is a good teacher," Fuller said.

"If I can buy my place back I'd like to go back to Rainbow Peak. Open up a school and hang my guns up forever."

"I made arrangements with Eddie for you to do that if you came back," Fuller said. "He'll keep a tract for watching over the place while we were gone, but the rest is yours."

"What about White Hair," Digger said. "Can you forget about him?"

"Time to put the past in the past and move on," Billie Jo said. "I lost the money you gave me somewhere along the way, Judge, was afraid to tell you. But I'll still pay you back somehow."

"I don't want anything back," Fuller said.

"What am I supposed to do," Digger said.

"You and the Judge can build us another ranch," she said.

Fuller and Digger looked at each other but didn't say anything. Digger looked back at Billie Jo. Fuller smiled at them.

"You two thought about what you want to do next?" Fuller said.

"We're thinkin' on it," Digger said.

"We're dressed for wedding. As a judge, I could marry ya'll here and now."

"I'm ready for whatever Billie Jo wants," Digger said.

"Marry me and we'll figure the rest out," Billie Jo said.

"What! Did you say what I thought you did?"

"Yep."

"I don't know what to say."

"Say yes," she said.

"Sure, I mean, yes," Digger said.

"Well," Fuller said, looking at Billie Jo.

"You're right, Judge, we are dressed for it," Billie Jo said.

"Well this could be the best day ever for you two," Fuller said. "I'll get some paper and write you out some marriage licenses after I perform the ceremony."

"Make it legal, Judge," Billie Jo said.

"I need to get a ring, don't I," Digger said.

"We'll get one later," she said. "Let's do it."

Fuller stood up and motioned for the two to hold hands.

"I'll make it short," Fuller said. "Do you take each other to be man and wife?"

"I do," they both said.

"Then I now pronounce you man and wife. You may kiss your bride."

Digger took Billie Jo in his arms and kissed her passionately.

"People are staring at us," Billie Jo said, blushing.

"Let them. I'm the luckiest man in the world," Digger said.

After some celebratory drinks, the three were talking in the hotel.

"We'll get some horses and guns and take off for Rainbow Peak tomorrow," Fuller said. "I can't wait to see Warren's face when we ride in. Why don't you go on up to your room. I'll make out a marriage license and we can all sign it tomorrow and get going."

"Best thing I ever heard," Digger said, threw his new Stetson up in the air, swiped Billie Jo off her feet and headed for the stairs.

Fuller picked up his knife and fork and cut his steak. He knew Billie Jo was finally happy. He smiled and took a bite.

# 31

The next morning, the Far West blew its whistle and woke Digger up. He rolled over in bed and discovered Billie Jo was gone. He jumped up, put his clothes on and scampered down the stairs and met Billie Jo coming up the stairs.

"There you are. I thought our marriage was over already."

"Don't be silly," Billie Jo said. "I had to get some ridin' clothes."

"What time is it," Digger asked.

"Almost noon. You were snorin' when I left. Here's some of the Judge's money to buy horses, guns and supplies. Why don't you go take care of that while I get a bath and put on my clothes."

"You think spendin' that money will be alright with him?"

"Sure, he lets me do what I want to."

"That was before we got married," Digger said.

"Don't worry about it. Go buy what we need," she said.

"Okay, when I get back I'm takin' them clothes right back off you."

"When the time's right," she said and smiled.

"Women got their own time."

"Men don't care what time it is if they can find a place," she said and Digger laughed. Billie Jo started back up the stairs and Digger walked down the stairs to the saloon.

Judge Fuller was sitting at a table with the same three men he was playing cards with the day before, sailors from the Far West with matching caps and beards, tattoos covering their arms.

Digger walked up to the table.

"Where's Billie Jo?" Fuller said.

"Takin' a bath," Digger said.

Fuller nodded. "Sounds about right. You want to join us?"

"I was goin' to buy what we need to go back to Rainbow Peak. Wanted to make sure it was alright with you, seein' how it's your money."

"She's training you already, huh," Fuller said. "You're gonna find out it takes a women a long time to get ready for anything."

The three card players nodded in agreement.

"You comin' with me," Digger said.

"Nope, I trust you," Fuller said. "You do it."

"Okay," Digger said and walked away.

After Digger had left, Fuller and the men played a few more hands before a white-haired man in a Union uniform—with captain's bars and a Seventh Cavalry patch on his coat, about Fuller's age, and missing his right leg—came rolling himself in the saloon in a wheelchair. He pulled up to a table across from Fuller and the bartender brought him a bottle of whiskey and poured a full glass.

Fuller continued to play cards but the more he thought, the more he thought about the man that murdered Billie Jo's mother. It wasn't likely, but he fit the description and the unit.

He waved the dealer off for cards, stood up and went over to the captain's table.

"Pardon me, Captain, were you at Sand Creek in sixty-four?"

The captain looked up at Fuller. "Ain't none your damn business, mister."

"I was there during the war. Name's Captain Fuller Newton."

"Guess you know 'bout Custer," the captain said.

"Yeah I know," Fuller said.

"Name's Seth Miller. And, yeah, we were fightin' the Cheyenne there in sixty-four. I commanded the second company of the Seventh."

"You have the white hair then?"

"Born with it."

"You remember murdering women and children?"

"No, we fought a brave battle."

"Against women and kids," Fuller said. "Never thought I'd see you again. I was there, in another company, after you butchered them and ran."

"You're wrong, mister, I never murdered anyone."

"I saw you runnin' down the mother of a little eight-year-old girl. You murdered her when you ran your sword through her. You got away before I could catch you, though. That little girl was a Union soldier's daughter. She's here now, and she's been lookin' for you all her life."

"You ain't frightenin' me, mister. Ain't no woman gonna kill me." He threw his coat back and was holding a pistol pointed at Fuller.

"Go ahead," Fuller said with a laugh. "You have no idea how well she can use a gun."

The captain didn't move, just looked at Fuller, studying him, and drank his glass of whiskey. Finally, he put the pistol in his belt, covered it with his coat and rolled his wheelchair out of the saloon.

Fuller walked back to the card table and sat down. "Deal me in," he said.

"Ante up," the dealer said.

After a dozen or so hands, Fuller looked through the smoke-filled room into the mirror on the far wall, then quickly looked again.

Pervez, the gunslinger Warren hired in Rainbow Peak, was walking up to the bar, a leather nose cast protecting what had been smashed by Fuller.

Pervez saw Fuller in the mirror and turned around. "Been lookin' for you," Pervez said. He drew his Colt and pointed it at Fuller.

"I don't have a gun, Pervez, I'm unarmed."

"Don't make no difference to me," Pervez said. "I'm goin' to kill you fer what you did to me."

"I thought you were a fast draw. Better that way than murdering me. Let me get a gun."

"Don't think you can beat me but I still ain't takin' no chances."

The bartender disappeared from behind the bar. The three card players gathered up their money and moved away from the table. The biggest of the three, named Tacker, was the only one wearing a gun. He moved over beside Fuller.

"This ain't any of my business," Tacker said, "But to shoot an unarmed man down in cold blood just ain't right."

"This ain't none of your business," Pervez said. "Back off or I'll take you down, too."

"Tacker, go on, he'll kill you," Fuller said.

"Well now, you finally givin' me some respect, but that don't change nothin'," Pervez said.

Tacker moved into a crouched position.

"You an ugly bastard with that leather nose," Tacker said. He went for his gun.

Pervez drew and shoot Tacker in the heart before his hand even reached the Colt. Tacker fell dead on the floor, his gun fell out of its holster and blood pooled around him. Pervez twirled his Colt one time and dropped it back in the holster.

"You other monkeys want to die," he said, looking at the other two card players.

They started shaking their heads no, moving slowly toward the door. Pervez stomped his boot and they took off running out the door and he broke into a laugh.

"Back to you, Judge. You see the gun on the floor. I'll let you go for that at the count of three. If you don't, I'm going to shoot you anyway."

"I believe you would," Fuller said.

Pervez nodded. "One."

Fuller jumped to the floor, snatched up the gun and turned to fire when Pervez shot him twice in the chest before he could get the gun in position. He dropped the gun and rolled over on his back. He didn't move.

Pervez holstered his Colt. "Bartender," he said, "get your ass over here and pour me a drink."

The scrawny bartender rose up from behind the bar, picked up a whiskey bottle and a glass and set them in front of Pervez, his hands shaking as he poured the drink.

A few people from the hotel came in to see what happened and quickly ran back out when they did.

Pervez leaned back against the bar, gulped his whiskey down and sat the glass on the bar.

"Needed killin', see what he did to me," he said, grabbing the leather nose cast, then poured another drink.

Digger was returning to the hotel and saw a crowd outside the saloon. He walked up to one of them he recognized. "What're you doin' out here?"

"A man in the saloon with a leather nose shot your friend," the man said.

Digger ran into the saloon and saw Fuller on the floor. He grabbed him up in his arms, checked his heart and looked up at Pervez holding a glass of whiskey.

"I'm celebratin', Digger. Want a drink? Finally got even with the Judge."

"You sorry bastard," Digger said. "He should've killed you and Warren back in Rainbow Peak." He noticed Tacker lying there, dead, too.

"Oh, I took care of Warren for you," Pervez said. "He wouldn't pay me what he owed me after that ruckus with the Judge."

Billie Jo came running in.

"I heard gunshots," she said.

She stopped when she saw Fuller, screamed and ran to him. She sat down beside him and grabbed his body from Digger.

"Oh, god, no," she said.

"C'mon, Billie, he's dead," Digger said.

"Well, well, if it ain't the little Indian whore," Pervez said and drank down his whiskey.

"I remember you," she said, wiping her tears with her sleeve and looking at Pervez. "You're the scumbag that worked for Warren. Think you're a fast gunslinger, huh? Got the guts to go against me in a gunfight?"

"I don't want to kill you, split-tail, but if you want to die I can accommodate you. Take that belt off the dead man, real slow now, and put it on. Holster that Colt, then you'll be ready to die."

"No, Billie Jo," Digger said. "We'll get the law."

"She's got more guts than you do," Pervez said.

"You know I have to do this, Eli, move back out of the way," Billie Jo said.

Billie Jo unbuckled Tacker's gun belt and took it off of him. She picked up the Colt with two fingers and looked at the cylinder, but couldn't tell if a round was in the firing chamber. She stuck the gun in the holster and strapped it on over her new pants and tied the holster down.

"You look kind of silly wearing that gun, almost hate to kill you. If you draw I'm goin' to."

"You go first," Billie Jo said. "I want to enjoy watching you die."

She stepped out in the center of the floor and Pervez straightened up from the bar. He reached for his gun and before he could clear leather she shot him between the eyes.

Pervez dropped the Colt and fell face-down, smashing his face on the floor, knocking his leather nose cast across the floor, blood running out of his nose and from between his eyes.

She stuck the Colt back in the holster and let the belt drop to the floor and walked back to Fuller, sitting down beside him again. She took his hand and sobbed. Digger sat down beside her and put his arms around her and let her cry.

After a good cry, Digger put Fuller on his shoulder and carried him to his room. Arrangements were made for Fuller at the undertakers and Digger went to see Captain Marsh for a ride as far as they could go on the river before transporting his casket the rest of the way to Rainbow Peak in a wagon.

Billie Jo was packing her dress and other things when she found her pa's badge, with the hole in it, and Fuller's old hat he swapped out when they got new ones.

She heard Digger open the door and walked up to him and put her arms around him.

"The Far West is goin' all the way to New Orleans," he said. "Captain Marsh said we could ride as far as we can go on the boat and get a wagon to go on to Rainbow Peak. I knew you and the Judge would want to take Bittersweet. The captain was very understanding about it."

"I think the captain liked the Judge," Billie Jo said. "No one else could have got that horse on the boat."

"You're right about that," Digger said. "When Bittersweet is ready we'll breed her to an appaloosa, hope for a colt and name him Judge."

"I might be ready by then, too." Billie Jo puckered and kissed Digger on the cheek.

"I'm always ready," he said and returned the kiss.

Billie Jo smiled and turned back to her packing.

"The Judge was like a father to both of us, but I think he would have liked it better to be thought of as a protector," Digger said.

"Yeah, I think so, too," Billie Jo said. "The Judge will enjoy the ride."

"You're not ever goin' to let him die are you?" Digger asked.

"No, he'll always be alive in my heart and on my mind."

THE END

# ABOUT THE AUTHOR

John L. Lansdale was born and raised in east Texas. He is married to the love of his life Mary. They have four children. He is a retired Army reserve psychological operations officer and a combat veteran that served three tours in Vietnam with numerous medals and awards. He is a graduate of a Texas police academy and a state certified peace officer. He is an inventor, country music songwriter, performer and television programmer. He produced the television special "Ladies of Country Music" and several other programs. He goes back to the Sun Record days and was introduced to Elvis Presley by Mary on their first date when Elvis was a seventeen-year-old student at Humes High School in Memphis and a ticket-taker at Loew's State Theater.

John has produced a variety of albums and music videos for country artists in Nashville along with songs for movies, with one as recently as 2018 titled "Tremble" for an upcoming film. He has hosted his own radio shows and won awards for radio and television commercials. He was a writer and editor for a business newspaper. He has worked as a comic book writer for Tales from the Crypt, IDW, Grave Tales, Cemetery Dance and many more. He co-authored Shadows West and Hell's Bounty with his brother Joe. He is the author of Slow Bullet, the four-part Mecana detective series, Long Walk Home, Zombie Gold and several others.

John's novel Slow Bullet was reviewed by Publishers Weekly as a must read page-turner with constant action and compared his work to that of popular 1950s author Mickey Spillane. The novel Long Walk Home was a finalist in the fiction category for the National Indie Excellence Awards. The novel Zombie Gold received great reviews including a Booklist review that praised it as a superb story with characters that came alive. Kissing the Devil received praise as a pulp novella. All titles are still in print with new ones on the way.

John was recently inducted into the Gladewater Museum. **His motto is: *Never Give Up.***

# AUTHOR'S NOTE

It's time I recognized and said thanks to my editor and friend Austin Holt. He has been a loyal, smart, skilled editor for most of my books. I don't know what I would have done without him. He helped me bring all of them to life through hard work, imagination and a trained eye determined to prepare them for an outstanding publication. I write them. He fixes them. I will always be grateful for his help.

# THE MECANA SERIES BY JOHN L. LANSDALE

All titles available individually or compiled in *The Complete Files of Detective Thomas Mecana* compendium.

HORSE OF A DIFFERENT COLOR - Book #1

Dallas PD Detective Thomas Mecana is on the hunt for a serial killer terrorizing the Lone Star State. Joining him is Darcie Connors, a young officer working her first murder case. With hard work, and some luck, Mecana and his partner discover a most-unusual serial killer case with murder in its very genes.

WHEN THE NIGHT BIRD SINGS - Book #2

Detectives Thomas Mecana and Darcie Connors are on the trail of a new suspect. With an ever-growing suspect list, Mecana must toe the line between friend and foe. Each action leaves them sitting in the crosshairs of danger. One wrong move could mean the end.

TWISTED JUSTICE - Book #3

Dallas Homicide Detective Sunday Verves is looking into the suspicious deaths of local drug runners when she discovers a potential suspect that hits too close to home. When the trail leads her south of the border, she enlists some old friends to track down the suspects.

THE BOX - Book #4

Detective Thomas Mecana and the gang get back together for another case. Mecana soon finds the case is bringing back old evidence. This horror-filled novel brings the Mecana Series full-circle to where it all began.

# OTHER TITLES FROM JOHN L. LANSDALE

SLOW BULLET

Army veteran Clark McKay is searching for the truth behind his best friend's murder. This search takes him across the globe, where he meets a multitude of characters and is forced to wade through the murky Washington DC waters of corruption. Clark McKay wants to find a murderer... but what happens when he uncovers so much more?

LONG WALK HOME

The O'Rourke family lives on a fading farm in the small town of Angel Point, Mississippi. With family, friends and neighbors fighting overseas in WWII - and rising racial tensions back home - the summer of 1944 turns into a nightmare of murder and loss. Trenton O'Rourke reflects on those days and how his life was forever changed.

THE LAST GOOD DAY

As the Civil War draws to a close, Major Rance Allison is wounded in one of its last battles. He later awakens in an enemy field hospital only to find out he is now on the same side as those he was fighting. The war is over. Missing a limb, his home and his family, Rance sets out to find a new life for himself.

BOY AND HOG / BOY AND HOG RETURN

In the deep woods, anything can happen. A group of white-collar workers with a hand-drawn map trek into the wilderness for a hunting expedition. But out there, will they be the hunters or the prey?

EMERGENCY CHRISTMAS

Join the Albright family and the guest who surprises them just in time for the holiday. Along the way, they discover sometimes crisis brings a family closer together.

# JOHN L. LANSDALE TITLES AVAILABLE FROM BOOKVOICE PUBLISHING

-Broken Moon (Hardcover - eBook)
-The Last Good Day (Hardcover - eBook)
-Long Walk Home (Hardcover - Paperback - eBook)
-Beyond Imagination (Hardcover - Paperback - eBook)
-Kissing the Devil (Hardcover - Paperback - eBook)
-Slow Bullet (Hardcover - Paperback - eBook)
-The Complete Files of Detective Thomas Mecana (Paperback - eBook)
-Horse of a Different Color (Hardcover - Paperback - eBook)
-When the Night Bird Sings (Paperback - eBook)
-Twisted Justice (Paperback - eBook)
-The Box (Paperback - eBook)
-Zombie Gold (Paperback - eBook)
-Emergency Christmas (Audiobook - Chapbook - eBook)
-Hell's Bounty [with Joe R. Lansdale] (Paperback - eBook)

STAY CONNECTED
WITH
BOOKVOICE PUBLISHING
AND
JOHN L. LANSDALE

www.bookvoicepublishing.com